P9-CAE-767

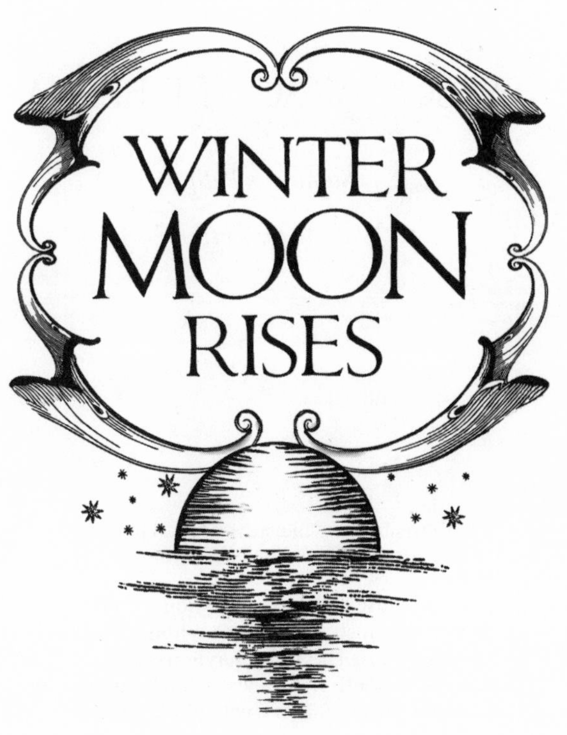
WINTER
MOON
RISES

ALSO BY SCOTT BLUM

Summer's Path

Waiting for Autumn

The above are available at your local bookstore,
or may be ordered by visiting:

Hay House USA: **www.hayhouse.com®**
Hay House Australia: **www.hayhouse.com.au**
Hay House UK: **www.hayhouse.co.uk**
Hay House South Africa: **www.hayhouse.co.za**
Hay House India: **www.hayhouse.co.in**

scott blum

HAY HOUSE, INC.
Carlsbad, California • New York City
London • Sydney • Johannesburg
Vancouver • Hong Kong • New Delhi

Published and distributed in the United States by: Hay House, Inc.: www.hayhouse.com • ***Published and distributed in Australia by:*** Hay House Australia Pty. Ltd.: www.hayhouse.com.au • ***Published and distributed in the United Kingdom by:*** Hay House UK, Ltd.: www.hayhouse.co.uk • ***Published and distributed in the Republic of South Africa by:*** Hay House SA (Pty), Ltd.: www.hayhouse.co.za • ***Distributed in Canada by:*** Raincoast: www.raincoast.com • ***Published in India by:*** Hay House Publishers India: www.hayhouse.co.in

Editorial supervision: Jill Kramer • *Project editor:* Alex Freemon
Cover design: Amy Rose Grigoriou • *Interior design:* Pam Homan

The Rumi poem on page 189 was translated by Andrew Harvey.

Library of Congress Cataloging-in-Publication Data

Blum, Scott.
Winter moon rises / Scott Blum.
p. cm.
ISBN 978-1-4019-2717-2 (hardcover : alk. paper) 1. First-born children--Fiction. 2. Mind and body--Fiction. 3. Spirituality--Fiction. I. Title.
PS3602.l864W56 2011
813'.6--dc23

2011024060

Hardcover ISBN: 978-1-4019-2717-2
Digital ISBN: 978-1-4019-3093-6

14 13 12 11 4 3 2 1
1st edition, November 2011

Printed in the United States of America

FOREWORD

I am very honored to write a Foreword for this brave, strange, and magical book by my friend Scott Blum. I am also especially honored to appear in it and give what little wisdom I have found on the Sacred Feminine.

I am not aware of such a book ever having been written before. This work has a unique and modern theme—that of a man who longs to be a father but is overwhelmed with despair and dread when he discovers that everything isn't as he imagined. This despair and dread take him into a depth of genuine inquiry and openness to revelation that leads him to all his own self-doubts and to a wholly new vision of what

Sacred Masculinity can be in a time like ours. So this book is at once a memoir; a thriller; a mystical confession; and a new kind of conversation about the nature of the Masculine and its responsibilities to the worship, adoration, and protection of the Divine Feminine in the great work of our time—the restoration of the full splendor and power of the Sacred Marriage in all of us.

If this sounds grandiose, it is my fault. Why the book works so movingly is that the story is such a human, gritty, and down-home story that opens quite naturally to its own supernatural dimensions. Scott Blum's great courage is to open us very simply and without artifice to his own growth and healing visionary journey; and to do so from the center of life as a man who owns a business, celebrates his marriage, works deeply on his inner life, and is trying to devote all he is to his heart's vision. It is Scott's sincerity that carries us throughout this ordinary and extraordinary story; and this sincerity is one of the heart and soul . . . and so is a very treasured gift between writer and reader.

May you enjoy this book as much as I have, and find its discoveries as I did.

— **Andrew Harvey**
the best-selling author of *The Hope*

Morning dew,
the clover glistens no more.

In afternoon.

CHAPTER ONE

Martika was the first person we told.

In her kitchen. The very same kitchen where Madisyn and I had first met.

Everything seemed oddly similar to the way it had been on that initial evening. Madisyn was dressed in a flowing pastel skirt that matched her silk-wrapped sandals; and I was once again wearing faded blue jeans, a T-shirt, and canvas tennis shoes. But it was our friend's kitchen itself that brought back the most vivid memories from several years before. The sweet smell of herbal teas danced with the nutty aroma of freshly roasted cashews, and stacks of self-help books crowded the fine china in oak cabinets. It was always comforting to visit the heart of Martika's home, and it felt like a perfect place to share our news for the first time.

"I'm preg—" Madisyn barely uttered the first syllable before the entire house filled with Martika's excitement.

"I knew it!" shrieked Martika as she plucked a rhododendron flower from a vase and placed it behind my wife's ear. Madisyn's wavy blonde hair gracefully framed the fuchsia petals, and I was once again taken by how much she resembled our close friend. If I didn't know better, I would have assumed that Martika was Madisyn's older sister because of their matching locks and petite stature.

"I could tell the first moment you walked in the door!" continued Martika, after wrapping my wife in a firm embrace. "How far are you along?"

"Five weeks."

Martika's smile remained as she waved her finger in a mock accusatory gesture.

"I know, I know," said Madisyn. "But you're basically family, and if you can't tell family . . ."

"I'm sure it'll be just fine," reassured Martika, her giddiness returning. "Do you want some tea?" she asked rhetorically while removing three china cups and matching saucers from the top shelf of a glass-faced cabinet. After putting a kettle of water on the stove, she unrolled a narrow bamboo mat on the table between us, carefully wiped the cups and saucers with a soft red cloth, and gently rested them on the mat. She then retrieved an ornate china pot, added two generous scoops of loose black tea from a golden cylinder, and slowly transferred the boiling water from the kettle to the pot.

I had seen Martika prepare tea in this manner twice before on special occasions, and Madisyn and I both watched in silence, appreciating the simple beauty of the ritual.

While the tea was steeping, Martika deliberately rotated each gold-rimmed cup handle to the three o'clock position. The dark liquid swirled as she poured the water into the cups, and the loose tea leaves floated counterclockwise at the surface.

Once the tea had all been poured, she looked at me and smiled knowingly before breaking the silence.

"Scott, I'm dying to know," Martika began. "Is it *her?*"

We all knew who she was talking about, and it was the only thing I had been able to think about since I had seen the matching plus signs on the pair of white plastic sticks. I'd had a strong connection with my unborn daughter since before I met Madisyn, and found myself regularly communicating with her in my dreams. And although my wife and I had both been anticipating her arrival during the past several years, we had decided to focus on our careers before having children, which made the news even more exciting when the day finally arrived.

"Of course it's Autumn," I asserted confidently. "She's been waiting patiently for years, and when she saw that the window was finally open, she flew right in."

"How does that make *you* feel?" Martika asked Madisyn.

"A bit left out, but I think I'll get used to it. I'd better, huh?" Madisyn laughed. "Every daughter goes through a *Daddy's little girl* phase, right? This one just seems to be starting a bit earlier, that's all."

It was true that I'd developed a stronger relationship with Autumn than Madisyn had, although I was pretty sure that the pregnancy would even the score by the time it was over. However, I was sensitive to the fact that having a relationship with our unborn child for many years before she was incarnate didn't exactly start the journey on an equal footing with my wife.

"So are you ready to become a daddy?" Martika asked me, her eyes twinkling.

"I'm not sure—I don't know. I guess so."

"It's natural to be nervous," Martika replied. "Conception, birth, and death are the three most important events in each of our lifetimes. And the former is probably the most special because it is so intimate. It involves only the souls of the mother, father, and baby—it's the ultimate expression of family."

"Yeah, I guess so. However, I would have expected a much stronger connection with Autumn now that she's closer, but she's been unusually silent since the beginning of the pregnancy."

"You haven't communicated with her?" Martika seemed surprised.

"Not recently." I sighed. "Sometimes I wonder if I've imagined this whole thing—if we simply made a baby like everyone else."

"The first thing to remember is that conceiving a baby is not the same as creating a baby from nothingness," Martika explained with a familiar sparkle in her eye that emerged whenever she shared her vast metaphysical knowledge. "Every baby's soul has *always* existed, and as new parents, you are just inviting it into your life. But it's the initial process of a child choosing its parents that I find most fascinating."

"Are you sure a child chooses its parents and not the other way around?"

"I'm absolutely sure. By the time a child is invited in, the parents are already well on their way down their own karmic paths of this lifetime. But at the beginning, a child soul only possesses a single unopened envelope of karmic debt, which is used to comparison-shop for parents. The soul essentially is looking for parents who have the most compatible karmic currency to help pay down this karmic debt."

"Karmic currency and karmic debt?" Madisyn interjected. "We sound more like a bank than prospective parents. Maybe I don't fully understand what karma is and how it works."

"Similar to the scientific law of gravity, karma is an *absolute* spiritual law that governs the nature of cause and effect," Martika replied. "Simply put, if we do something bad to someone else, our karmic debt increases. If we do something nice, it gets paid down."

"Isn't that the same with everyone you meet?" I asked. "What makes the relationship of a parent and a child any different?"

"Our karmic debt works hand in hand with our soul contract—the agreement we make with the universe before we're born about what we need to accomplish during this lifetime. These are usually core lessons we need to learn about relating to ourselves and other beings on this planet. For example: compassion, greed, family, anger . . . that sort of thing. So let's say a key lesson we need to learn in this lifetime is compassion. If our parents have a nice, easy life, providing us with anything we need or could want, we might not be in a position to learn *why* we must be compassionate to people less fortunate than ourselves."

"We wouldn't be able to relate," I noted.

"Exactly. But if our parents' karma provides for a lifetime of financial struggle and they're unable to provide us with the basic needs of food, shelter, and clothing, we would have a much deeper understanding of why compassion is an absolute necessity in this world."

"So having a difficult childhood isn't necessarily a bad thing."

"Not from a karmic perspective. It might be exactly the foundation that allows us to pay down our karmic debt and learn our core life lessons."

"Well, I hope that Autumn has already learned compassion," said Madisyn. "I don't want to have to lose everything we've earned just to teach her a lesson. But I guess since she's been hanging around so long, she's probably the only one who wants us."

"Unlikely. If you consider that every living being has a soul, there are literally millions dying each day. For every conception, it's likely that there are thousands of souls waiting in line to be reborn. It's just that Autumn's karma is perfectly matched with your own."

"Who would've thought that making a baby could be this complicated?" I said with a wry grin. "I think I learned the abridged version in elementary school."

"I know what we should do!" Martika exclaimed suddenly. "Meet me here tomorrow afternoon and bring some comfortable walking shoes. I know the perfect way to honor the beginning of the most amazing journey you'll ever have . . ."

As Martika walked us to her front door, I had the distinct feeling that everything was oddly different than it had been when we first arrived. The pungent food smells were deeper and more complicated. The precarious stacks of books were suddenly flirting with gravity as we walked by. And the paintings appeared to have taken on additional brushstrokes while we were having tea.

Yes, everything did seem oddly different—precisely because it *was* different.

Nothing would ever be the same again.

CHAPTER TWO

"Everything is going to be just fine," I said softly while driving along the country road toward Martika's house. The stately ranchlike estates were a welcome contrast to the more densely clustered dwellings of downtown Ashland, Oregon; and although it was only a few minutes' drive between our houses, it often felt like we were going on vacation whenever we went there.

"What are you worried about?" I asked.

"There are so many things that can go wrong. I just don't know if it was a good idea to wait so long," replied my wife.

"We needed to wait until the business was stable enough to support everyone."

Madisyn and I had started a company together, and it had taken a few years before it was able to sustain itself. We weren't the first to discover that nurturing a start-up takes a lot of time, money, and energy, although we were lucky that it was eventually able to support all the people who were relying on it.

"I know, I know, but I'm just feeling we might have waited too long."

"We're still young," I said confidently. "We might be older than some of the other parents, but we'll make up for it in experience."

"It's different for boys," my wife noted sadly. "Girls are taught from a young age that they only have a limited time to have children."

"Oh, that's not true anymore. It's very common for women to have healthy children well into their fifties now." I didn't want to discount her feelings, but I honestly believed she was overreacting based on an obsolete societal pressure.

"It's a feeling I've had since before we got pregnant," she said, gazing out the passenger window as we pulled into Martika's driveway. "I just hope everything will be okay."

Martika was waiting for us next to her car and hugged us both tightly after we parked. "Come on, you guys," she said excitedly. "We don't want to be late. You can ride with me . . . Onyx is already in the car."

The front passenger seat and floorboard of Martika's white Subaru station wagon were filled with dozens of used astrology books, so we both climbed into the backseat next to the full-grown black Lab.

"Hi, Onyx!" Madisyn said when she got inside. "Are you ready for a walk?"

Onyx panted excitedly and attempted to climb up on our laps. The backseat was roomy, although it felt cramped with the overzealous dog.

"Settle down, Onyx!" Martika yelled from the front seat. "Sorry about the passenger seat. I forgot to go to the bookstore to drop these off earlier—they also have another boxful for me to pick up. I'm completely obsessed with astrology at the moment. It's absolutely fascinating how accurate it all is . . . I resonate with it completely."

"It's okay," replied Madisyn as she scratched the side of Onyx's muzzle. "It gives us a chance to catch up with this handsome guy."

"Do you ever miss him?" Martika asked me as she headed toward the mountains, in the opposite direction of town.

"Yeah, I do miss him," I said sadly. Onyx looked at me wistfully. "But Madisyn's cat, Zoe, would never have allowed him to stay. She barely tolerated me when I first moved in."

Onyx had originally been the companion of a dear friend of mine named Robert whom I had met when I first moved to Ashland. Robert taught me many things about life and was essentially responsible for my own personal spiritual awakening. When he was preparing to move on, Robert had requested that either Martika or I take care of Onyx after he was gone. The dog stayed with me for almost a year until I moved in with Madisyn, and then he began living with Martika, where he'd been ever since.

"He's one of the best things that ever happened to me," said Martika. "I'm the luckiest girl in the world to be able to spend my life with this incredible soul. I'm so happy I was able to get my allergies under control, because I can't imagine living a day without him."

Looking out the car window, I realized I had never continued up the road past Martika's house. The curvy lane narrowed as it meandered up into the mountains, deep within the forest above the Rogue Valley.

"Where are we going?" asked Madisyn.

"It's a secret," Martika replied with a childlike giggle, "but I think you're going to like it!"

We continued up the gravel mountain road until we came to a small turnout that was already occupied by a white Subaru station wagon. Martika parked behind her car's twin and quickly got out and opened the doors for us. Instantly, Onyx leaped out of the backseat and ran up the path and waited for us on the ledge.

"I guess *he* knows where he's going," said Madisyn.

"Onyx and I walk up here at least a couple of times a week," agreed Martika as she collected a canvas Co-op bag from the floorboard, next to the pile of books. "I think it's his favorite place on Earth."

Madisyn followed Martika, and I trailed behind on the narrow pathway. We hiked up the steep incline for several minutes, with Onyx running in front and waiting at a bend for us to catch up, then happily darting ahead. When we finally reached the top of the hill, Martika paused to allow us to enjoy the vista, which was unlike anything I had seen before in Ashland.

The terrain was distinctly junglelike, as the path ahead appeared to be suspended above the dense forest floor by slender conifers that stretched high into the clouds. Massive shafts of golden light shone through the branches and landed on the well-worn trail like giant yellow spotlights, while millions of golden particles sparkled within the sunbeams themselves. But most unusual was the density of the air—even our breath felt heavier and palpably softer than it did in town.

"Absolutely magical," Madisyn gasped. "How could I not know about this place?"

"There are many hidden gems around Ashland," said Martika. "The town is deceptively small, but the magic within is endless."

The three of us hurriedly traversed the forest path to keep up with Onyx, and once we eventually made it to the crest of the third plateau, the Lab was patiently waiting for us with his front paws crossed.

On our left was an imposing void carved deep into the face of the granite mountain, which resembled a gaping mouth with an insatiable appetite for anything that would dare to walk near it. There was also something disarmingly alive about the depths of the cavern itself, as if the inky shadows inside were undulating and dancing with one another.

"Here we are," said Martika as she gestured toward the cave.

"I'm not going in *there!*" exclaimed Madisyn. "I didn't bring a flashlight!"

As if on cue, the shadows within the cave began to coalesce, and a mysterious woman gradually emerged from the darkness. She had long snowy-white hair and was wearing a reddish-maroon velvet dress that was adorned with several strands of exotic gemstones draping from her neck. The blood-hued velvet cloth dragged on the ground and completely covered her feet so that she appeared to float into the space in front of us.

Martika and the mysterious woman embraced, kissing each other lightly on the lips before Martika introduced us: "Madisyn and Scott, this is one of my dearest friends, Caroline. She has prepared a very special ceremony for Madisyn today."

Caroline walked up to Madisyn and tenderly held both of her hands and looked deep into her eyes for what seemed like hours. Madisyn's incredulous expression immediately melted into a blissful smile, and I could sense that my wife became more relaxed than she had been since finding out she was pregnant. Caroline then squeezed Madisyn's hands and said in a soft voice, "So nice to see you again, my child."

My wife continued to smile at the unfamiliar woman, and I instinctively held my breath while waiting for her to acknowledge me. Caroline then silently floated in front of me and placed her right hand on my shoulder. I was startled by a current of electricity that flowed from her jewel-encrusted fingers down the length of my arm. She then looked directly into my soul with her piercing emerald eyes. I felt like I was sinking into a bottomless pit, deep within the center of the earth.

"Mr. Scott," she finally said aloud as her lips pressed into a gentle smile, highlighting the deepest wrinkles around the corners of her mouth and eyes. The lines revealed lifetimes of wisdom that were intimidating at first glance. "Today we will be performing a sacred ceremony that is traditionally for women only."

My heart sank when I heard these words.

I would have graciously encouraged Madisyn to attend any women-only ritual if I had known about it ahead of time, but after feeling the energy of the moment, I was disappointed that I wasn't going to be able to share it with her.

After a long silence, Caroline slid her hand down my arm and squeezed my hand firmly. "But we have much work to do, don't we, Mr. Scott? I have made the appropriate preparations to welcome you into the sacred feminine space for today only. However, you must remain in silence and be mindful of your place as a guest. Do you understand?"

I nodded as Caroline turned to Madisyn and asked, "Are you ready?"

Madisyn smiled as she followed Caroline to the opening of the cave with slow, deliberate steps.

Caroline gestured for her to wait as she removed a long braided bundle of sweetgrass from a wicker basket that was waiting at the entrance. She then proceeded to ignite one end of the braid with a match. The air quickly filled with a sweet pungent cloud, and she began to *smudge* Madisyn by systematically waving the bundle around the perimeter of her body until every inch had been covered with the blue-green smoke.

"Wait just inside the entrance," Caroline whispered, and Madisyn disappeared into the dark cave.

Caroline then extinguished the smoldering bundle on the ground and produced a large, well-used bundle of white sage. After lighting the new bundle, she smudged Martika and me in the same way.

The cave was much larger than I expected, and while we were waiting patiently for Caroline to smudge herself, my eyes began to adjust to the flickering candlelight that illuminated the cavern. Nearly a dozen glass votives were nestled into the crevices of the smooth stone walls, and in the center of the cave was a small round table that was covered with an embroidered red velvet cloth. Perched atop were six unlit candles—three large pillars and three medium-sized tapers held erect by a trinity of antique pewter bird-claw candlesticks. Resting at the feet of the shimmering talons was an *athame,* an intimidating silver dagger with an ornately carved ebony handle.

When the mysterious woman finally entered the cave, all of the candles appeared to dim, and a pronounced chill filled the air. It was as if she commanded all of the oxygen in the cavern and the flames were struggling to stay lit in her presence. I absentmindedly rubbed my arms for warmth through my thin sweater as I watched her mouth move in a silent prayer.

Caroline removed a candle from the wall and walked into the center of the room, gesturing for us all to remain where we were. She placed the votive on the altar and then ceremoniously cradled the dagger with both hands and lifted it high above her head. She brought the *athame* to her lips and kissed the shining blade. I felt a rush of energy fill the room as I watched her deliberately use the knife to carve a large circle into the dirt around the perimeter of the cave.

She purposely left a narrow opening in front of Madisyn and beckoned her and Martika to enter, making it clear that I was not welcome to join them. I did my best not to take it personally, although there was still a part of me that felt I should be allowed to stand next to my wife and be an active participant in the ceremony.

Once the women were inside, Caroline closed the circle with her dagger and returned it to the altar. She used the candle from the glass votive to light each of the three large pillars, which corresponded in color to the smaller tapers in front of them—red, white, and black. Caroline then moved Madisyn to the center in front of the red candles. Martika was positioned to the left in front of the white ones, and she herself returned to the right side in front of the black ones.

"I call forth the Triple Goddess to join us on this auspicious day," Caroline announced in a booming voice that filled every inch of the cavernous space. "Maiden, Mother, Crone, you are within all of us sisters on this earth; and you give us each strength from the power of the moon. As spring into summer, and summer into winter, and winter into spring again, you fill us all with the exquisite beauty of your grace.

"Today we are here to celebrate *Maiden* Madisyn as she transforms into *Mother* Madisyn and follows her own divine path of the Triple Goddess. The mother is represented by the full moon, which will provide Madisyn with the essence and energy she needs while embracing motherhood. Her new role is that of the nurturer, and she will be responsible for tending to the seeds and dreams that have been planted within her family. Home and hearth will be the foundation that will bring her strength, security, and resolve during this sacred journey."

Caroline then removed a single sheet of square yellow paper and a red pen from the opposite side of the altar, and handed them to my wife.

"Madisyn, I encourage you to write down any fears you may have about your new role of motherhood."

Madisyn laughed nervously. "I don't think that's enough paper."

"Just write down what you can." Caroline smiled.

Madisyn began writing intensely, and in less than a minute had filled the front side of the paper. She flipped over the page to fill the back with little effort. She then turned the yellow sheet sideways and continued writing in the margins until there wasn't any room left.

"I guess that's enough." Madisyn sighed, returning the page to Caroline. "I hope I remembered everything."

With the deftness of an origami master, Caroline carefully folded the yellow sheet into a small cone and gently placed it upright on the altar in front of the center candles. She then removed the black unlit taper from the holder and gestured for Madisyn and Martika to remove the tapers immediately in front of them. Once all three women were holding their candles, Caroline lit her own from the flame of the black pillar candle and slowly walked to Martika's side before speaking in a clear, deliberate voice.

"Of the divine circle of the Triple Goddess, the Maiden receives the flame from the Crone." Once the candle was lit, Caroline kissed Martika on both cheeks and returned to her place to the right of Madisyn.

Martika then turned to Madisyn and said, "Of the divine circle of the Triple Goddess, the Mother receives the flame from the Maiden." She then lit Madisyn's candle with hers and kissed her on both cheeks, smiling lovingly.

Caroline then turned to Madisyn and said, "Madisyn, the flame of motherhood that you now hold in your hands burns brightly with the collective fire of the Maiden, Mother, and Crone. You will never be alone on your new journey, and you can always draw from the strength of your sisters."

In the flickering candlelight, I could see the shimmering path of tears as they made their way down my wife's cheeks. At that moment a blanket of energy swaddled me, and I hastily removed my sweater, as the temperature in the cave seemed to warm in a matter of seconds.

"It is now time for you to release your fears of motherhood," Caroline continued in a gentle voice, gesturing for Madisyn to light the paper cone with her candle. Once she did so, it burst into flames and quickly burned to its base. After it had nearly burned completely, the charred remains of the cone magically rose up from the altar and floated toward the ceiling. The beauty of the floating ash was incredible, and when it had disappeared from view, I joined the others in a chorus of gasps that filled the space. Caroline then brought the taper to her lips and blew gently to extinguish the candle. After replacing it in the holder, she gestured for the other two women to follow her lead.

Once the three tapers were no longer burning, Caroline walked directly in front of Madisyn; looked deep into her eyes; and said in a soft, loving voice: "Welcome to motherhood."

The commanding tone returned to her voice as she turned to the altar. "Dearest Triple Goddess, thank you for blessing us on this auspicious day. When you are ready, please depart in peace with our everlasting gratitude. Return whenever you desire, for you are always welcome."

She then extinguished the three pillar candles, and when the last one was snuffed, the cave fell to darkness and the electricity present in the air since we had entered instantly evaporated. When my eyes finally adjusted to the darkened cave, I saw that Caroline was quickly shuffling around the perimeter of the circle, erasing the line clean with her feet.

"That was wonderful," Madisyn said, embracing both Caroline and Martika at the same time. "I feel very supported right now."

"You are, my dear," replied Martika as they made their way out of the cave.

I followed behind the women until we had reentered the forest, and then I walked up to my wife. Her face looked different in the golden twilight—stronger and more confident. "I'm proud of you," I said, hugging her tightly. "You were very beautiful in there."

"Is there anything we can do to help clean up?" Martika asked Caroline.

"No, I can manage. You all go home, and Madisyn, you would be best served to rest for the next few days—you'll want to integrate all the new energies that you have received."

The three of us had started up the path toward the car when I remembered that I had left my sweater inside the cave. Caroline was waiting for me in front of the entrance with my cardigan in one hand and a piece of paper in the other.

"You should call me," she uttered in a solemn voice as she handed me the handwritten note. "I see something in your field that concerns me—you may need some help."

CHAPTER THREE

That night I had the latest in a series of anxiety dreams that had begun as soon as Madisyn got pregnant. They always focused on my childhood, although in this one I was much younger than in most.

I stood in front of a local circuit judge flanked by my mother and her new husband inside a linoleum-floored courtroom. The fluorescent lights reflected off the imposing paneled bench separating the judge from the three of us, and our voices echoed as if we were inside a stone cavern.

"It says here that the child's father has been remiss in paying support for quite some

time," the judge said in a booming and authoritative voice.

"That is correct," replied my mother solemnly.

"And that you and your new husband wish to adopt this child and be legally responsible for all of his needs, financial and otherwise."

"We do."

"What is the child's name? Ah yes, I see it right here. Mr. Scott—"

This was the first time in my life anyone had called me "Mr.," and it made me feel quite important. I instantly warmed up to the judge.

"—do you understand what it means to be adopted?"

At seven years old, there was no way I could truly understand all the implications of adoption, although I did my best to parrot the speech my mother had prepared me with.

"It means that my last name will change so when my new daddy picks me up from school, they will let him take me home because we will have the same name."

"That's true." The judge laughed. "He's a precocious little boy, isn't he? Is that what you want, Mr. Scott?"

"Yes," I responded as confidently as I could. "I want to be 'dopted."

"Who can argue with that?" The judge laughed again. "You will receive a new birth certificate within the next four to six weeks that will have the new father's name on it. I will also order the existing birth certificate with the previous father's name to be legally sealed for the life of the child. From this date forward, nobody will be able to obtain any official document with reference to the preceding paternity."

The next morning I stayed in bed while I mulled over the emotions the dream had stirred up. Being adopted hadn't changed anything from my perspective at first—other than that I had a new last name to play with and was able to discard my old one with all the ceremony of an empty candy-bar wrapper. In one fell swoop, adoption made the inconvenience of mismatched surnames a thing of the past. One day I was a Saxton, and the next I was a Blum. Simple as that.

As the years progressed, I gradually lost touch with my birth father, although the adoption couldn't explicitly be blamed for that. He was busy with his new family, and we ended up living well over a thousand miles away from each other. Every few years we would reconnect, and we even managed a few visits during my adolescent years, but his consuming guilt and my growing indifference always seemed to make our visits more awkward than I intended.

However, the adoption itself had a much more insidious effect on me. I never genuinely felt connected to the paternal side of my bloodline because of the confusion of where my loyalties should remain. I felt loved and cared for by my entire family, but I never felt like I *belonged.* And after my sister was born, the connection to my mother's side diminished as well. On the surface my family was a cohesive unit that was as traditional as apple pie, but underneath I felt like I was the only one who remembered that I didn't fit in.

But now I was in the midst of trying to bring another soul into this world, into *my own* family, and I didn't even know what family *I* belonged to. For the first time in my life I felt completely cut off from my own bloodline—the very one I was attempting to pass on to my child.

For the first time in my life I felt truly orphaned.

"Have you given any thought to Autumn's last name?" I asked my wife, noticing she was also now awake.

"A bit," she responded coyly.

"I don't know—I just feel weird about giving her the name Blum. It's not really *my* name, you know?"

"That's a relief," Madisyn replied. "Because there's no way I was going to agree to that."

"Why not?" My feelings were hurt, although I had already conceded the point without her asking.

"Because of exactly what you said—it's not your name."

"Okay." It made much more sense when I was thinking about it myself, but it somehow felt uncomfortable when she said it.

"I was thinking she could take *my* name." She smiled. "Autumn Taylor."

For some reason, this felt even worse to me. There was a part of me that felt excluded, as if I wasn't part of the family at all.

"What about me?" I asked. "Then I'd be excluded from her life completely."

"Don't be ridiculous—you'd still be her father. And if it means that much to you, why don't you take my name as well? Scott Taylor." She smiled again. "That has a nice ring to it."

"No," I said firmly, without even considering her offer. "I gave my last name up when I was adopted, and I *won't* do that again."

"Well, if that's the real issue," she replied perceptively, "then why don't you change your name back to Saxton?"

She was right—that was the real issue. "I don't know about that. I think it would really hurt my parents' feelings."

"Don't you think it hurt your birth father's feelings when you changed it the first time?"

"Of course it did. But that was years ago, and I was only seven years old. Why should I dig all of that up again? Shouldn't I just let well enough alone?"

She shrugged.

"But what about Autumn?"

"What did you think of Caroline yesterday?" Madisyn always knew when it was time to change the subject.

"I thought the whole experience was a bit intimidating." I surprised myself by saying it out loud.

"Powerful women are always intimidating—especially for men."

"Maybe that was part of it, but I just didn't feel like I belonged there."

"I think she made a very real effort to make you feel welcome. Besides it was a *women-only* ceremony, and you weren't even supposed to be there."

"That's exactly my point. I just don't feel like I have an inherent bond with *any* group of people."

"What do you mean?"

"In today's world, nearly every group of people seems to have a shared bond within itself. Women, African Americans, disabled, gays, and so on. The only group that doesn't seem to have an intrinsic bond with one another is *straight white males*. Can you imagine what would happen if someone created a support group for straight white males?"

Madisyn laughed. "That's because straight white males have historically been responsible for oppressing everyone else."

"I know, and evidently that's my burden to bear."

"I don't think anyone is going to feel sorry for you."

"And they shouldn't—it's just that I feel lonely in my *straight white maleness* sometimes."

"Perhaps it's time for you to finally embrace your Native American heritage. If I had Indian blood, I'd be at every powwow within a hundred miles."

Madisyn was right. My great-grandfather was responsible for the majority of the Cherokee blood flowing through my veins, and there was something about bringing a new baby into the world that made me want to reconnect with my ancestral line on an even deeper level.

"Maybe that's it. I should probably keep my eye out for an event that resonates with me."

"I'm sure that will help," she said compassionately. "So, what did Caroline give you when you went back to get your sweater?"

"Her phone number. She said that I needed help, and I should call her."

"Well, you better do it," Madisyn replied in a serious voice. "Martika said that Caroline isn't taking any new clients . . . so if she's offering, it's probably pretty important."

"What does she do?"

"Martika speaks highly of her work—some kind of soul healing, I think. I'm not sure exactly what she does, but you should find out."

We spent the next few hours leisurely getting ready for the day. The weekends gave us the chance to be together as a couple, since much of the time during the week we needed to play the role of business partners. After bathing, I dug through the pockets of my jeans and handed Madisyn the crumpled note that Caroline had given me. She studied the handwriting for a few seconds and started dialing the number without saying a word. She then handed me the receiver before it began ringing. Caroline answered after the first ring.

"Um, hello. It's Scott from yesterday. Martika's friend."

"Hello, Mr. Scott," Caroline said matter-of-factly. "I just had a cancellation a few minutes ago. I'd like to see you at one o'clock today."

CHAPTER FOUR

When I arrived at Caroline's house, I was surprised to find that the entire property was fenced in by tall wooden planks. The green paint was in the final stages of peeling, and on the gate was a sign that read: BEWARE OF DOG. I wasn't sure if I should let myself in, but when I reached for the latch, the thunderous barking that ensued gave me my answer.

I looked through a knothole near the bottom of the fence and saw a large German shepherd with bared teeth that was responsible for the intimidating noise. In the distance I glimpsed Caroline float-walking toward the gate to let me in. After standing up and dusting off my knees, I tried to look as calm as possible in the presence of Canine the Protector.

The gate was flung open, revealing Caroline, who was wearing a green velvet dress and a single strand of amethyst gemstones. She smiled warmly and extended her arms to embrace me fully. Her presence was profoundly calming, and I felt a warm tingle of energy coming from every place where our bodies met through her soft velvet dress. She was definitely good at hugging, and my heart sank ever so slightly when the embrace ended too soon.

"Come on, Mr. Scott. We have a lot of work to do."

"That's quite a dog you have," I noted.

"Oh, that's Shasta. He's my receptionist. He screens all my clients and tells me what to expect before I see them."

I suddenly felt self-conscious and wondered if I'd made a mistake by looking at him through the knothole. "Did I pass?"

"You wouldn't be in here if you didn't." She laughed.

Caroline's lot was much larger than it had appeared from the street. A small forest of densely planted trees and bushes crowded the small cottage that was set in the middle of the property.

As we walked through a breezeway attached to the house, a much quieter Shasta left us alone, entering a makeshift doggy door to the right of the screened entryway. We continued to the backside of the house, where a padded massage table was set up on the bank of a tiny babbling brook.

The feeling was utterly magical, and I couldn't help but notice the fairylike sparkles glimmering on the surface of the flowing water. As I squinted, the diamonds of light transformed into shapes vaguely resembling dragonflies floating lazily down the stream.

"Good . . . you can see them."

"See who?" I asked.

"The elementals. They were all excited when they heard you were coming today. Martika told me that you could see spirits . . . especially your unborn daughter."

"I don't always *see* her," I explained. "Sometimes I just hear her . . . or feel her. But that all seems to have changed since Madisyn got pregnant."

"I understand. Please remove your shoes and lie faceup on the table—let's see if we can contact her today."

I felt a tingling of excitement in the pit of my stomach as I lay on the padded table. It didn't occur to me that someone else could connect with Autumn, and although it wouldn't be the same as communicating with her directly, I was excited about the possibility of being able to check in with her.

On my back, I couldn't help but revel in the sensory abundance that filled Caroline's property. The soothing sound of the trickling brook instantly calmed my mind, while a gentle breeze softly caressed my entire body with its delicate touch. Immediately above me was one of the most glorious trees I had ever seen. It towered confidently far above the house, clutching thousands of tiny pink flowers that all but obscured the green foliage.

"Just relax," Caroline said in a soft voice. "I'm going to start by reconnecting your energetic meridians."

She pressed one strong index finger firmly below my shoulder blade and held it there for several seconds. She then brought her other index finger next to it and gently followed the edge of my torso until she found the bottom of my rib cage. Once she found the precise location, she pressed hard with her second finger, and I felt a faint electrical charge travel between the two fingers along the path she had traced. Surprisingly, when she removed her fingers, the electrical charge remained, as if she had unblocked a channel that was now able to flow freely.

Caroline repeated the process on the opposite side of my torso; and then continued with my arms, legs, and many other points throughout my body. Although the process was inherently energizing, it was also profoundly relaxing.

In my altered state, I was vaguely conscious that she had finished reconnecting my meridians, and afterward she tenderly placed her hands under the back of my head and firmly pressed her fingers into my neck. She held me in that relaxing pose for several seconds before gently pulling on the base of my skull, and I felt the warm breeze begin to surge and swirl around me. The howling gust sounded like a tropical storm as it blew through the branches of the trees and shook the windowpanes with its insistent force. I wasn't sure if I was imagining it or not, but in my dreamlike state, I felt myself being lifted off the padded table and float into the sky above.

Although my eyes were still closed, my mind was filled with a series of vivid images of Mount

Shasta from various perspectives. The noble mountain just south of the Oregon-California border was easily the most prominent natural landmark for hundreds of miles. It had always elicited a sense of wonder from me, ever since I'd first seen it at the age of twelve when our family had moved to the area. The bright pink sunsets illuminating the snow-covered cliffs embodied an exquisite beauty that rivaled the most picturesque tropical beaches. And the saucerlike lenticular cloud formations contributed to its magical reputation among both nature lovers and woo-woo New Agers alike. I had never scaled its summit, but many of the images I saw in my mind's eye that afternoon were clearly from a perspective at the top of the peak that I couldn't remember having seen in a photograph.

"Mr. Scott . . ." I heard someone whispering my name from what sounded like another room. "Mr. Scott, it's time to return . . ."

When I opened my eyes, I saw a single blue dragonfly hovering above my face, before it darted into the cloudless sky. At first I assumed I must have imagined the bout of inclement weather until I noticed that the tree above me had been thoroughly stripped of its pastel-colored flowers. I involuntarily brought my hand up to scratch my nose when I noticed that I was covered in a blanket of the soft pink petals.

Caroline leaned over me, her face upside-down. Her jaw appeared to be hinged from the top and moved like a surreal marionette when she spoke.

"How do you feel?" she asked with her oddly inverted mouth.

"Um, okay, I guess. Sort of disoriented, I think."

"It will take a few minutes to integrate—just relax."

"The flowers . . . the wind . . ." For some reason my mind was unable to construct full sentences, as if my vocabulary had temporarily been diminished.

"Yes, the nature spirits were quite active during your session—you had a lot of help today."

Part of me was relieved that I hadn't imagined the entire session, although it definitely created more questions than it answered. However, one stood out far above the others. "Did you see Autumn?"

"Oh yes. Autumn is quite the little spirit, and she shines with a light that is *very* bright. However, there is still one thing that concerns me."

"Concern? *Still?* What do you mean?"

"One of the main reasons I invited you here is because I saw something very unusual in your energy field yesterday."

"What is it? Am I okay?"

"Oh yes, you are definitely okay. How do I say this?" She paused for a few moments while collecting her thoughts. "When a woman is pregnant, it's not only her body that grows to accommodate the fetus. It's equally important that her soul also increase in stature to allow the baby's *spirit* to feel safe as it transitions into human form."

"Like a spirit womb?"

"Yes, that's a good name for it. During the gestation process, newborns don't spend the entire time within their own bodies—in fact, they spend much of it in the spirit world, where they were residing before the pregnancy. Of course they explore their new home on occasion, but most of the time when a child soul is near its mother, it remains in the *spirit womb* because this feels more natural."

"I think I understand," I replied to Caroline's marionette mouth. "But what does that have to do with me?"

"Ah, that's the thing. When I met Madisyn yesterday, it was obvious that her spirit womb was progressing nicely. But remarkably, you also appeared to have your own spirit womb that was even further along. That's what I wanted to explore today. And it appears that Autumn is very comfortable in *your* spirit womb and has been visiting it for quite some time."

"I don't understand. What does that all mean?"

"To say it another way"—she smiled an upside-down frown—"congratulations, Scott, you're pregnant, also."

My mind was reeling, and I wasn't sure how I felt about the news I had just heard. "Is that common?"

"I've never seen it before. The spirit womb is inherently a feminine phenomenon. I've never seen a father with one before."

"Is that bad? Am I hurting her somehow?"

"I don't *think* so," Caroline said in an unsure voice. "In fact, she seems exceptionally happy and healthy."

"What about Madisyn?"

"That is the most remarkable thing. Even after I explained that Madisyn is carrying her, Autumn still believes that *you* are her mother. She calls Madisyn the *other mother.*"

"How could this happen?"

"That's exactly what I'm trying to figure out. As far as I can tell, it seems as if it was Autumn's choice. Most people have soul contracts with their children well before the parents are even born. It's an agreement between souls that is usually based on what they can teach each other when they incarnate."

"Martika explained that to us."

"Good. But what's strange is that according to Autumn, you made the agreement with her well *after* you entered your current physical body."

"Do you think it was when I first started dreaming about her, around the time I met Madisyn?"

"I don't know . . . let me ask." Caroline closed her eyes and went quiet for several seconds before resuming our dialogue. "She tells me that it was long before you met the *other mother.* Did you live in this area many years before meeting Madisyn?"

"Yes, I did. In Yreka, just south of the Oregon border."

"That makes sense. She showed me pictures of Mount Shasta, where she had been waiting for you for many years."

A chill went down my spine as I recalled my visions during the session. "I wonder if that's one of the reasons I ended up back in this area."

"Undoubtedly."

"But why can't I communicate with her like I used to? If she's so close, wouldn't it be easier?"

"She wanted to know the same thing. She thought you were ignoring her, but I reassured her that it wasn't true. Mothers are supposed to develop a bond with their babies when they are in utero so the survival instincts can take over at birth. That's why so many mothers have dreams about their babies when they're pregnant even if they don't usually communicate on a soul level. Therefore, the interdimensional dialogue is primarily limited to the baby's biological mother during pregnancy.

"It's sort of like a highly evolved form of spiritual genetics that keeps the conversations focused on building the maternal relationship. Because I work with a lot of pregnant mothers, I'm able to bridge the worlds more easily, but it will be nearly impossible for you to communicate with Autumn while she's still in the womb."

I was saddened to discover that I wouldn't be able to speak with Autumn until after she was born, but I was also encouraged to find that she would be able to spend some quality time with Madisyn so they could get to know each other. "Could you tell her that I miss her and I'm looking forward to meeting her in person?"

Caroline closed her eyes and was silent for several seconds before responding in a strange, childlike voice: *"We'll be together very soon."*

CHAPTER FIVE

After my trip to see Caroline, my anxiety dreams became much more frequent and vivid. Many of them stemmed from my early teenage years when our family moved from Los Angeles to the northernmost tip of California. We settled in a small town called Greenview that had exactly fifty-three residents, a post office, a gas station, and of course, a bar. Tucked between the Marble Mountains and the Trinity Alps, the town served as the belly button of the picturesque farmland known as Scott Valley. At first I was excited that we had moved to my namesake, but in less than a year I began to despise the entire valley and especially dread the twenty-minute bus ride to and from school. . . .

"Why do you always wear that necklace?" Jim quipped as he plopped onto the green vinyl seat next to me.

"I dunno," I replied, still unsure why my Southern California fashion acumen seemed to attract so much attention from fellow students. Everyone in my previous school had worn puka-shell necklaces, but evidently I was the only one in my new school to own one.

"Because it looks like you stole it from your momma's jewelry box. Do you always wear your momma's jewelry?"

I tried to ignore him the best I could.

"And why do you wear girl clothes? Can't your parents afford to buy you your own clothes?"

He then reached into his faded jeans and pulled out a large black-handled pocketknife. With a flick of his wrist, the blade scissored open and gleamed in the sunlight that shone through the bus window. The weapon had serrated teeth halfway down the blade that looked like they could easily saw through bone.

"Maybe I should gut you like a buck." He laughed as he mimed the shape of a cross with his knife. "Put you out of your misery."

I looked up at the bus driver and noticed that his eyes were on the road for once. He was always looking in the large mirror above his head to keep the "precious cargo" in check, but for some reason on this day he decided to watch where he was going on the desolate two-lane highway.

"Don't say a word." Jim had stopped laughing. "Or I will gut you."

He pushed me forward and slammed my forehead into the back of the galvanized-metal seat in front of us. I felt the shell necklace dig into the soft flesh of my throat. As he sliced the fishing line that held it together, dozens of tiny pukas scattered on the floor, rolling down the aisle.

"Now look what you've done." He laughed. "You gotta be more careful with your momma's jewelry!"

Within seconds the bus filled with crunching noises as dozens of enthusiastic feet began stomping on the shells. My favorite necklace was reduced to thousands of tiny shards in a matter of seconds.

"No joke," Jim calmly whispered as he again flashed the angry weapon and returned it to his pocket. "Like a buck."

As the bus rolled into the school parking lot, I squeezed my eyes shut tightly so my tears would remain locked inside. Thanks to my "fashion consultant" and his razor-edged assistant, I learned a valuable lesson that day:

Boys don't cry.

After waking up, I wasn't able to get back to sleep. I knew that girls had different challenges than boys, but I began to doubt if I was truly ready to be responsible for a child's emotional safety.

If I was still upset by what had happened during my own childhood, how could I be a parent to somebody else?

CHAPTER SIX

The next few weeks were filled with repeated visits to the doctor that gave me a crash course in the medical aspects of pregnancy. By the time we were nine weeks along, Madisyn had already endured multiple ultrasounds and several appointments with a team of professional "blood-suckers." At first the ultrasound was interesting, but after repeated viewings of the blurry peanut on the screen, the invasive procedure began to lose its charm.

"I don't know about Dr. Carducci," I said to Madisyn as we were driving away from the doctor's office after another round of blood tests had been scheduled.

"Why not? I think she's nice."

"Yes, she's nice, but she hasn't exactly honored your request that this be a natural experience."

"She's just being extra careful because of my age."

"I think she's relying on traditional medical procedures to protect herself from being sued. Maybe we should ask around to see if we can find a good midwife. Do you really want to have the baby in a cold hospital anyway?"

"I didn't, but I'm starting to feel that the doc has a valid point about having the extra support in case something goes wrong. And besides, they do have a water-birth center at the hospital, and she says we can play any music we want during labor."

I was surprised that my wife was defending Dr. Carducci, given how opposed to traditional medicine she had been the entire time I'd known her. But I understood that this was a scary time for her, and ultimately she was the one who needed to feel most comfortable with whatever path we were taking.

"And besides," Madisyn continued, "I'm still worried that the *spotting* might turn into something bad."

"Even the doc said that's probably nothing to worry about." I tried to reassure her.

"I know, but she also said it's possible—"

"Okay," I interrupted as gently as I could. "If you feel comfortable with the doctor, then we'll stay with her."

"I think it's a good idea," my wife said as we pulled up to our shared office. "Let's get back to work so I can try to get ahead before Autumn arrives."

The next morning Madisyn woke up utterly exhausted and wasn't able to get out of bed the entire day. Fortunately, it was Saturday, so I was able to stay at home and take care of her without having any other obligations to attend to.

At first we thought it was simply a normal case of morning sickness, but as the day progressed, her spotting had turned bright red and her abdominal pain had come to be nearly unbearable. I was finally able to convince my wife to let me call the doctor around 9:00 P.M., although we knew it was unlikely she'd be able to see Madisyn on the weekend. We had to jump through hoops to persuade the answering service to page the doctor on a Saturday night, and she finally returned our call after several minutes that seemed like hours.

"Hello, it's Dr. Carducci."

"It's Madisyn's husband, Scott. Madisyn isn't doing too well—could you come and see her?"

"What's wrong?"

"She's in terrible pain. Her abdomen is killing her . . . and she's starting to bleed a lot!"

"She should go to the emergency room," the doctor said firmly.

"That's what I suggested earlier, but she doesn't want to go to the hospital. Is there anything you can call in for the pain until we can see you?"

"They can give her what she needs at the emergency room." Dr. Carducci was getting impatient. "I'll call the hospital to let them know to expect you. Go now. Do you need me to call an ambulance?"

When she mentioned an ambulance, it finally sunk in how serious it was. Even though I'd been trying to convince Madisyn to go to the hospital for hours, hearing the doctor's adamant directive made me feel that I should have insisted earlier.

"She said that we need to go to the emergency room immediately," I told Madisyn, after hanging up the phone.

She resisted at first, but when I explained that the only other option was to call an ambulance, she begrudgingly agreed to let me guide her to the passenger seat of my car. The ten-minute drive was noticeably uncomfortable for her, and at every stop sign the pain appeared to escalate to another level. By the time we arrived at the hospital, my wife had been writhing in pain for so long that it took a bona fide effort to untangle the seat belt before I succeeded in unlatching it.

She was barely able to shuffle to the hospital entrance with my help, and with every step during the short journey to the waiting room, her pain intensified, as did her guttural moaning. Fortunately, the obstetrician was true to her word, and the admitting nurse was expecting us, a manila folder of paperwork in hand. I was able to fill out the insurance forms very quickly, and we were whisked into a private room to wait for the emergency-room physician. I then helped my wife into a flimsy gown and tried my best to comfort her when she curled into a fetal position on the examining table.

We were in the linoleum and stainless-steel room for what seemed like an eternity before a young male nurse showed up with a clipboard. By that time, Madisyn's veins were visibly protruding from both sides of her flushed neck, and she began to shake uncontrollably while he proceeded to ask her the same questions I had already answered for the admitting nurse.

"So why are you here tonight?" he inquired in a calm voice while Madisyn's legs were involuntarily kicking.

"Dr. Carducci told us to come to the emergency room immediately," I replied. "She's pregnant and she's bleeding and she's obviously in a lot of pain! Can you please give her something for the pain?!"

"I would like the patient to answer," he said calmly as Madisyn ripped the white paper sheet off the padded table and let out a piercing scream. "Madisyn, when was the date of your last period?"

Surprisingly, Madisyn collected herself and retrieved the date from some part of her brain that wasn't preoccupied by the pain. She then answered the rest of his questions as coherently as she could in between the sharp stabbing pains that increased in intensity and frequency.

After the nurse finished asking her the obligatory battery of mundane questions, he then removed a laminated yellow card from his clipboard and showed it to Madisyn. It had six circles with simply drawn facial expressions representing a continuum of suffering on a scale of 1 to 10. It seemed absurd to resort to such a childlike tool when any preschooler would have easily deduced that if the face on the far right indicated a 10 on the pain scale, my wife was obviously registering at least a 15.

"On a scale of 1 to 10, what is the pain that you are feeling right now?" the nurse asked matter-of-factly.

"Ten," she said weakly while clutching her abdomen. "Can I *please* get something for the pain?"

"Yes, I'm going to recommend to the doctor that we give you something to make you feel better. He's with another patient right now, but he will be with you as soon as he's done."

Madisyn let out a frustrated sigh and closed her eyes tightly.

"Let me get you some ice chips," he continued. "I'll be right back."

True to his word, the nurse returned with a small paper cup containing a few ice chips that Madisyn was able to extract moisture from.

Over the next hour, Madisyn's situation progressed from bad to worse. During her episodes, it took nearly all of my strength to keep her on the examining table while she writhed in pain and her limbs thrashed independent of one another. The thin paper covering on the table had been ripped apart, much of it in large pieces of irregularly shaped confetti scattered on the floor. Fortunately, there were small breaks between her convulsions, although the reprieves became shorter as the night progressed.

I ultimately left the examining room during one of these breaks to seek out someone who might be available to help my wife. When I entered the hallway of the emergency wing, I was shocked to find that nobody was around. It was eerie how empty the hospital was, as several examining tables were wheeled up against the sterile walls, and rows of vacant desks had apparently been abandoned in the midst of work. The entire scene reminded me of being the last one out of an office building during a fire alarm. I briefly panicked that some tragedy might have struck while we were in the examining room, before I saw an orderly exiting the ladies' room.

"Can I help you?" she asked in a vaguely condescending voice.

By this time I was getting nervous about leaving Madisyn by herself in the room, and I heard the anxiety manifest itself by way of my constricted throat. "My wife is getting worse!" I yelled. "Can someone please come in and give her something for the pain! She's having convulsions now and is much worse than when we arrived!"

At that moment a bloodcurdling howl sounded from Madisyn's room, and I ran down the hallway.

"I'll find someone right now," the orderly called after me in a concerned voice as I shoved open the door.

Inside, Madisyn was practically naked as a result of her contortions, and the flimsy hospital gown was drenched in blood. I ran to the examining table and did my best to comfort her as she dug her fingernails deep into my arm while letting out a piercing scream that echoed off the lime-green linoleum. Her breathing became more erratic, and she eventually began hyperventilating between screams.

"It's okay," I tried to reassure her. "The orderly said someone will be right here."

Within just a few seconds, the first nurse we'd seen appeared at the door with a plastic bag of clear liquid suspended from an IV hanger. He quickly wheeled it next to Madisyn while I attempted to reclaim my wife's modesty by draping her legs with the blood-soaked gown.

"I'm going to start your IV so we can give you something for the pain," he said in a calm voice while attempting to hold her hand steady. "But you're going to need to be still so I can insert the needle into your vein."

Madisyn pulled herself away from the nurse and screamed loudly while writhing facedown on the examining table. By this time my own anxiety began to overtake me, and the lights appeared to dim as I desperately tried to turn my wife over onto her back. Watching her writhe in pain for hours on end was finally getting to me, and it took nearly all my resolve to remain "present."

The nurse put his face just a few inches in front of Madisyn's and squeezed her hand firmly while commanding her in an authoritative voice: "Breathe. Take a deep breath and *breathe* with me." He then took a deep breath himself and repeated, "I need you to *breathe* so we can get your IV started. Breathe in deeply . . . *one, two, three* . . . good. Now breathe out slowly . . . *one, two, three.* Good. Isn't that better?"

Remarkably, Madisyn followed his lead and began breathing with him until she started to calm down. I felt myself return to my body and began caressing my wife's hair while the nurse deftly inserted the needle into her wrist. Within seconds he had secured it with three layers of tape and attached a narrow tube to the suspended plastic bag. I found myself temporarily distracted from the reality of the situation as I watched the hypnotizing drip making its way from the bag to my wife's arm.

"Okay, try to be as still as possible so you don't rip out your IV," he said as he hurried toward the door. "I'll be right back with the doctor to give you something for the pain."

As soon as the door was shut, Madisyn contorted in agony, and her face turned a deep shade of purple, the veins in her neck protruding. She then began hyperventilating again and rolled onto her side, clutching her stomach. It took all my strength to keep her from rolling off the table, and whenever I tried to help her breathe, like the nurse had done, she dug her fingers hard into my arm and shrieked at the top of her lungs. By this time, my arm was so covered in blood that I wasn't sure if it was from her or if she had succeeded in puncturing my skin with her nails.

When the nurse once again returned without a doctor, I was ready to yell at him before he said, "The doctor requested that I start you on morphine immediately." He was carrying a tray of labeled vials that clinked against one another as he placed them on the metal table next to Madisyn's IV. He pierced one of the small bottles with a hypodermic needle and sucked out the clear liquid before inserting it into a plastic cylinder protruding from the IV tube.

When the drug entered her veins, Madisyn had a surprised look on her face and froze for a few seconds, before letting out another scream that seemed slightly less intense than the ones that had preceded it. The nurse reassumed his position in front of my wife and once again calmed her down by helping her breathe.

"Does that feel better?" he asked in between breaths.

"Uh-huh," she gasped. "A little."

The nurse produced the yellow laminated pain card and repeated, "On a scale of 1 to 10 . . ."

Madisyn interrupted him with an agonizing howl that rattled the vials of medicine next to the examining table.

"Okay, let me give you another dose," the nurse said while quickly preparing another syringe. "I started with a very small amount, so I'll give you a little bit more."

Although I was impatient about getting the pain under control, I was also thankful that he was being judicious with the drug. I had made a point of writing on the admission form that Madisyn was ultrasensitive to medication. Over the years I'd discovered that even a single tablet of over-the-counter pain reliever could leave her with side effects for days.

When the second dose entered her bloodstream, Madisyn let out an audible sigh, releasing the mountain of tension that had built up throughout the evening. The plum hue of her face lightened to a pale crimson almost immediately; and within just a few seconds more, faded to a flushed pink. For the first time in several hours I was able to recognize that the person writhing in a blood-soaked hospital gown was indeed my wife.

"Does that feel better?" the nurse asked softly.

"Uh-huh." Her voice was hoarse from screaming and sounded like she had just returned from smoking in a coal mine for twenty-odd years.

"Let's clean you up a bit."

After removing the red-stained paper from the table and the floor, the nurse retrieved a kidney-shaped bedpan from under a cabinet and filled it with warm water. He sponged Madisyn's legs to remove as much of the smeared blood as he could before she began tensing up again.

"It comes in waves," she croaked, while digging her nails into my forearm. The hue of her skin once again deepened to crimson as she let out another ear-piercing scream. Madisyn arched her back involuntarily, and her eyes rolled to the back of her head. "Owwwwww," she cried. "It huuurts . . ."

With a determined look, the nurse emptied a third vial of morphine into the tube, which rapidly produced the desired effect. "That should keep you for a little while. The intravenous meds work quickly, but they don't last very long—we should probably get some meds into your muscle tissue so they will last longer." He produced the laminated yellow pain chart and asked again, "On a scale of 1 to 10 . . ."

"Eight," Madisyn whispered after a long pause. Her eyes were no longer in the back of her head, and she began to breathe normally for the first time in hours.

"Are you okay?" I asked, gently caressing her tangled hair.

"No," she responded plainly. "But at least now I don't feel like I'm dying."

I still felt helpless, although I was relieved that she was able to speak coherently.

"Roll over on your side," suggested the orderly, who had prepared a fourth syringe. "I'm going to give you a shot of morphine into your muscle." He inserted the needle into the flesh below my wife's hip. Madisyn didn't appear to notice the injection at all, although I felt myself wince for her. "This will last much longer than the IV medication."

At that moment the doctor finally walked through the doorway. Harried green eyes complemented his frizzy white hair, which gave him the air of an annoyed professor.

"Sorry for the delay," the doctor said in a perfunctory tone, after retrieving the clipboard from the nurse. "But it looks like we were able to take the edge off while we were waiting—it's always busy during the full moon." He quietly cleared his throat while flipping through the pages of the clipboard.

"When was the date of your last period?" the doctor asked.

By this time I was used to medical personnel treating that particular question as a salutation, although it was difficult not to interject that she had already answered it twice since we had arrived.

Madisyn repeated the answer and patiently waited for the inevitable.

"Okay," the doctor said while sliding out a chrome-plated apparatus from under the examining table. "Put your feet in the stirrups and let's have a look-see."

After putting on latex gloves, the doctor began the invasive examination. I could never understand how even the most immodest woman could tolerate such procedures, especially from doctors they didn't even know. Thankfully, it didn't last very long, and within a few seconds he had finished and his gloves were in the white cylindrical repository under the sink.

"Have you had an ultrasound during this pregnancy?"

"Several."

"I think we should have another one to be sure," he said gravely.

The nurse followed the doctor out the door, and my wife and I were once again alone in the examining room. Thankfully the medication seemed to have temporarily diminished the pain, and Madisyn closed her eyes and rested while waiting for the next round of tests.

It was in that moment that my attention finally shifted from the immediacy of my wife's painful condition and came to rest squarely on the potential repercussions of what had happened. Until that moment it hadn't even occurred to me that Autumn might be at risk, although when I let myself take in everything that had gone on since we'd arrived at the hospital, it seemed obvious. Madisyn's legs were still streaked with blood, and her abdominal cramps were so severe that there only seemed to be one logical conclusion.

I closed my eyes briefly, and when I reopened them, the examining table appeared to float off the ground as the hospital room fell into darkness. I was standing at the end of a long tunnel, with my wife being wheeled away by a shadowlike figure I couldn't see. Her face was no longer visible, and the deafening sound of wind overtook the relentless clanging from the air ducts that had been in the background since we'd arrived. As the wind echoed in my mind, a sense of aloneness began to fill my soul, and a profound sadness washed over me. I felt myself falling backward, deep into the dark void around me, when I was startled by another voice in the room.

"Hello?"

The clanging returned, and the examining table was once again next to me. I instinctively went to my wife's side before looking at who was responsible for the greeting.

A tall woman with pink paisley scrubs was hunched over a bulky white machine with a head-like monitor growing out of its plastic swiveled neck. Her unkempt chestnut hair obscured her face, and her long fingers reached up to tuck the locks behind her ears.

"Hello?" she repeated in a soft, understated voice. "The doctor asked me to take some pictures."

Madisyn opened her eyes and blinked deliberately while the technician busied herself with wires and buttons until the robot machine sprang to life. She then covered a corded plastic wand in a plastic sheath and spread a generous amount of clear gel onto it.

"I apologize, but I'm going to have to ask you to put your feet back into the stirrups just a little while longer."

Madisyn reluctantly complied, and closed her eyes when she was in position. Within seconds the familiar ghostlike images began to appear on the ultrasound monitor, which undulated like a sky full of electronic clouds. Periodically the monitor would focus on a gray kidney-shaped figure surrounded by a thin white halo floating in the darkness. I recognized the embryo from our previous ultrasounds, but this time the figure didn't sparkle with movement the way it had when the former technician had pointed out the blinking heart pumping blood through the translucent body. This time the tiny organs remained motionless.

The technician outlined an array of pixelated boxes around the embryo and typed in various coordinates, then shut down the ultrasound machine. I had the distinct impression that she was trying to avoid eye contact as she wheeled the machine into the hallway.

Before closing the door, the technician fixed her gaze on Madisyn and whispered in a somber voice, "I'm sorry."

CHAPTER SEVEN

Madisyn was eventually released from the hospital after the nurse injected a final syringe of morphine for good measure. Once we arrived home, she fell asleep as soon as her head hit the pillow. I was also exhausted, although I couldn't get the black-and-white ultrasound images out of my head.

At first my mind raced with all the possibilities that kept my daughter "in the pink." Perhaps the ultrasound wasn't working properly or the technician had inadvertently misplaced the wand. Or maybe Autumn was simply resting. She was probably just practicing shutting down her heart in an exercise of embryonic meditation, like those cave-dwelling yogis in the mountains of southern India. That was probably it—just meditating. Or sleeping. We had all had a long night, and when it was picture time, she was most likely just tired.

Then I felt it.

It had been easy to avoid in the swirling chaos of the hospital, but within the stillness of our bedroom the feeling was unavoidable.

Nothing.

It started as a nearly imperceptible trickle from the right side of our bed. Within just a few short moments, the trickle begat a stream, and the stream begat a roaring river. An unmistakable void emanating from my sleeping wife's belly filled the room.

Absolutely. Nothing.

Although I hadn't been in communication with Autumn since she had entered my wife's uterus, there had still been a presence that I had taken for granted. In every fiber of my being, I had known she was with us every day. And although I couldn't speak with her in the same way I had in the past, I could still sense her soul. But now, my daughter was nowhere to be found, and I could no longer avoid the emptiness that pervaded the room.

It didn't take long before the *nothingness* had entered my body. It started by consuming the pit of my stomach and gradually slithering up the insides of my torso, numbing every organ one at a time, until even my heart and lungs felt like they were no longer of service. When it reached the base of my esophagus, it ballooned to the size of a beach ball and quickly consumed every inch of my throat.

As the ball swelled inside of me, I felt myself gasping for air, repeatedly trying to extract enough oxygen to breathe. As I flirted with unconsciousness, the bubble burst into a million pieces and forced its essence deep into every cell of my body. I felt *nothing* like I had never felt it before—a powerful, dark, consuming tarlike void. It emanated from every pore of my skin and leaked profusely from my eyes, skating down my cheeks and onto the bedsheets under my chin.

I quietly sobbed for what seemed like hours, powerless to move and scarcely able to breathe. The emptiness had encased me in a tightly wound cocoon that relentlessly squeezed every emotion out of my tear-soaked eyes.

And within that cocoon of emptiness, my world finally collapsed—I sank deep within the mattress and lost consciousness, before floating into dreamland. . . .

The crimson-azure sky welcomed me, as did the sweet smell of honeysuckle that filled the air. I stood alone atop a gently sloping knoll, perched high above a valley that reflected the twilight in soft shades of pink and purple. An exquisite breeze caressed my cheek, and as I looked up, a majestic raven began circling me in the sky above. The large black bird flew just close enough that I was able to glimpse her shining ebony eyes looking deep into my soul.

Sitting down with my knees to my chest, I watched as the raven circled above me for several minutes until she appeared to get bored and flew off into the distance. I then got up and lazily began walking along the crest of the knoll, vaguely following the direction in which the raven had flown.

Before long I came to a large plateau, and when I stopped, I heard a faint humming sound that seemed to sway in rhythm with the gentle breeze. Looking for a suitable place to rest, I absentmindedly hummed along as the sound gradually became louder and louder. Before I knew it, the sweet and gentle humming had crescendoed into a deafening chorus that enveloped my surroundings.

At first I wasn't able to discern precisely where the buzzing was coming from, but as I looked to the ground, I noticed that the grasses were alive with a movement that far exceeded what the breath of the wind could animate.

And then I saw them.

The ground was carpeted in an ankle-deep sea of honeybees extending for acres in every direction. Their yellow-and-black–striped bodies were so densely packed that I almost mistook them for the grass, thinking it was a few inches taller than it actually was. And although I was not allergic to bee stings, I couldn't help but let fear penetrate my thoughts and began to worry that this Army of Buzzers might grow angry.

Then immediately in front of me, thousands of bees gathered together to form a frenetic bell-shaped mound almost three feet tall. Once the bell was nearly solid, a humanlike figure began to emerge from the pile of bees, and within moments an auburn-headed little girl was standing in front of me. The insects had arranged themselves around her into the most perfect shape of a sundress, with a ruffled bodice and two narrow straps that appeared to hang the bee dress from her delicate, pale shoulders.

I instantly recognized my unborn daughter and was genuinely impressed with her fashion acumen.

"You sure know how to make an entrance," I said loud enough to be heard over the incessant buzzing.

Autumn stood in front of me with a sad expression on her face. It was the first time I had seen her when she wasn't happy, and it broke my heart. With a nearly imperceptible nod, she appeared to wordlessly urge the bees to "whisper," and within seconds the insect chorus had diminished.

"You were supposed to be the mother." My daughter's childlike voice had a decidedly accusatory tone.

"Madisyn is your mother," I said softly. "I am your father."

"You were supposed to be the mother," she repeated.

"I understand that it was confusing." I was finding it difficult to explain something that I didn't understand myself, but she deserved an answer. "In this lifetime, mothers are girls and fathers are boys. And I'm a boy—I can't be your mother."

She remained silent and stared at me intently for what seemed like hours. When it was obvious that I had nothing else to say, she finally uttered in a quiet melancholy voice, "I waited for you."

In that moment I felt wholly inadequate as a father and began to doubt that I was cut out for parenthood. Autumn believed that I had misled her somehow while she had waited in vain for years for me to become her mother. I didn't know how to explain what had happened, let alone how to make her feel better. I knew Madisyn truly loved her and that she would love Madisyn once she got to know her, but I couldn't help but feel my daughter's enormous disappointment. And when I was unable to come up with even a single word to comfort her, my heart began drowning in a pool of tears.

With a final nod, Autumn summoned a chariot of bees to appear around her and gently lift her off the ground. She slowly turned away as the chariot carried her far into the distance, floating gracefully above the sea of honeybees, which once again filled the air with their buzzing drone. Just before she disappeared over the horizon, she turned to me one last time and uttered something entirely unintelligible.

Then she was gone.

Autumn moon descends,
and darkness returns.

Silver remains.

CHAPTER EIGHT

"It was more than a week after the miscarriage before Madisyn was willing to see any of our friends. She was feeling understandably fragile and needed her time alone to process everything that had happened, which suited me just fine, as I was also going through my own emotional roller coaster. But she eventually agreed to see Martika at our home after a flurry of phone calls on an overcast Sunday afternoon.

"How are you feeling?" Martika asked after I led her to the living room, where my wife had been taking refuge for the past several days.

"Much better physically," Madisyn replied, wrapping her legs in the flannel log-cabin quilt my mother had sewn to celebrate our marriage. "But I'm afraid the emotional wounds will take much longer to heal.

"I keep thinking that I could have done something differently," my wife continued, after taking a sip of freshly brewed peppermint tea. "Maybe I should have started taking the prenatal vitamins sooner, or rested more instead of working so much. I don't know. I guess the main thing I keep thinking is that we waited too long . . ."

"Waited too long?" Martika asked.

"I'm not exactly a spring chicken anymore. I'd been telling Scott for years that my biological clock was ticking, but he wanted to wait until the business was bigger, more established—whatever. There was always some excuse, and after days of agony, I didn't even get the prize."

Madisyn was unable to suppress her tears any longer, and she finally cried for the first time since we had left the hospital. It was true that we'd had many discussions about her biological clock, but I felt with every fiber of my being that it was necessary to be financially stable before bringing a child into the world. I was raised on the cusp between lower- and middle-class America, and although my family never accepted government assistance, I always suspected this had more to do with my parents' pride than our not qualifying for it. We never wanted for food or clothing, but there were many times when having more significant financial means would have made life much easier.

But seeing my wife crying that morning made me feel that I might have made a life-changing mistake. It was true that I hadn't wanted to have a child until I believed that everything was "just right," but I never thought that by waiting, we would actually *lose* a child. In that moment I began to wonder if the miscarriage could have been my fault.

Was it possible that I was responsible for my daughter's death because of premeditated negligence?

"How many times did you try?" asked Martika.

"Try?"

"To have a baby. How many months before you became pregnant?"

"I got pregnant the first month." Madisyn wiped her eyes and smiled softly. "I'm a fertile goddess."

"In that case, I don't think that *you* are the issue," Martika replied confidently. "Most of the time the *child* is responsible for a miscarriage."

"The child? Do you mean that she might have had an incurable disease and couldn't survive the womb?"

"Perhaps. But more often than not the child *chooses* to terminate the pregnancy—exercising her own free will."

"How is that possible? And why would she do that?"

"Transitioning from the spirit world to the physical world is quite a dramatic shift. Even the most *un*aware babies must question their resolve to give up the freedom and beauty of the spirit world when they choose to join us on this planet. That's why the soul of a baby bounces in and out of its new body during the term of the pregnancy—it's trying to get used to all the unique rules of living here."

"But what about Autumn?" I asked. "She's been wanting to come here for years."

"Wanting to live with you two and being bound by the complicated rules of this planet are two very different things. I'm sure that Autumn is far from *unaware,* given the simple fact that she chose you two as parents. In fact she's probably *ultra*sensitive and found life in the physical world to be crass and severely limiting."

"I know I do," interjected Madisyn.

"And that doesn't even address the individual body itself," Martika continued. "Many baby souls try out several bodies until they find one that has the perfect balance of protection and sensitivity."

"Sort of like test-driving a car." I smiled.

"That's not funny," Madisyn said, shooting me a dirty look. I could tell that she wasn't amused by the implication that something created within the sanctity of her uterus could be so casually rejected.

"What about her soul contract?" I asked. "Shouldn't she have known what body she was destined for before she was even conceived?"

"Soul contracts are complicated." Martika sighed. "Yes, it's true that her *soul* knew what she was in for before her body was conceived. But part of what makes a soul contract work is that it relies on the inherent separation of consciousness from destiny. That is the bedrock of free will, which starts long before the soul enters the womb."

"You mean that Autumn didn't *consciously* know that she was going to reject the body before it was conceived?" I was trying to follow Martika's logic.

"Probably not."

"Well, I'm still mad at her," Madisyn said plainly. "I suffered through an unbelievable amount of pain because of her *little decision*—not to mention that it was dangerous. Do you know how much blood I lost?"

"That's understandable," Martika said soothingly while rubbing Madisyn's elbow. "But it's valuable to remember that the process of birth and death are *the* two most sacred experiences on this planet that one can share with another. And as a mother, you were in the unique position of being able to share both with her within a very short amount of time."

"But what was the point?" Madisyn asked sadly. "What possible good could have come of such a brief visit?"

"You gave your daughter the incredible gift of being able to work through some very important karma in a short amount of time. Most of us have to stay on Earth for decades before we successfully work through all the karmic responsibilities of living here. Autumn was fortunate that you agreed to allow her to work through the most significant karmic responsibilities of her lifetime while she was still in the womb."

"Well, good for her," said Madisyn flippantly, still obviously hurt. "But what do *I* get out of it?"

"You were able to learn the ultimate lesson that is at the core of all karmic experiences."

"What's that?"

"Love. There are very few experiences as powerful as a miscarriage that can strip karma down to its very essence. *From conception to our final resting place, love is the reason for being.*" Martika closed her eyes and let her words settle around us like golden leaves floating to the ground.

"No matter which lessons we're meant to learn in this life, they all come down to love. We need to move beyond our 'self' and learn that we are all one—we are interdependent, and love is the thing that nourishes our connection with one another. A mother can't help but understand this at the core of her being when she's growing a baby inside of her."

"She was a part of me," whispered Madisyn, her tears beginning to resurface. "There were times when I swear I could feel my own blood pumping through her tiny heart."

"And when a child is never born," Martika went on, "the only thing that remains is the love that nourished each of you during the brief time you shared."

"But if her karma is already fulfilled," I interjected, "is she going to come back?"

"The karma of *this* lifetime is fulfilled," clarified Martika. "Whether she comes back or not is yet to be seen. According to the *Tibetan Book of the Dead,* she will have forty-nine days to determine if her soul has learned enough to be *liberated,* or if she will be reborn again to learn additional karmic lessons."

"I don't know if I'll be ready to try again by then," said Madisyn. "And to be honest, I'm not sure I want to go through that again—*ever.*"

Hearing Madisyn say these words saddened me deeply. I couldn't imagine not being able to bring Autumn into this world—to hold her in my arms and rock her to sleep. Although I was anxious about the responsibilities of a parent, I'd been waiting to see my daughter in the flesh for many years, and the possibility that Madisyn might not be willing to try again filled me with sorrow.

"It's up for debate whether the forty-nine days are literal or symbolic," said Martika. "But we do know for sure that she will rejoin you if it's meant to be."

"You and your *meant to be.*" I attempted to force a smile. "Sometimes I wish *I* could be responsible for deciding what was going to happen in my own life."

"We all do," Martika whispered. "But like it or not, the destiny of our unborn children is permanently entwined with our own."

"I just assumed we wouldn't have to worry about being parents until after Autumn was born. But she's just so demanding—even in the spirit world, she seems to pull the strings."

"That's more common than you think—it's just that not every parent is tuned in to what's actually happening. But especially now that she had begun to incarnate, Autumn's influence on the physical world will be greater than ever. If I can give you a little advice . . . be sure you make peace with her now—or else you'll be sorry later."

I instantly got truth bumps down the back of my neck, as if the temperature in the room had dropped ten degrees. I didn't understand what she was talking about, but I knew I needed to find out more.

"Sorry? That sounds ominous—what do you mean?"

"As you know, I spend a lot of time with ancestral healing. At the core of much of that healing is attempting to honor everyone who has ever been involved in a family line—whether born or unborn. If a family member has been disowned or forgotten for whatever reason, all hope of a healthy and positive family line is permanently on hold until every member is acknowledged and openly honored, no matter what they may have done to deserve banishment. In other words, the *forgotten* will torment the *remembered* until everyone is openly acknowledged and allowed to return to their place."

"That sounds like superstitious voodoo," remarked Madisyn. "Do you honestly believe that's the case?"

"Yes," whispered Martika in a manner that seemed to draw darkened circles under her eyes. "Honestly, I do."

"Either way, I know that won't happen with us," I spoke up. "Autumn will arrive soon enough, so she can torment us in our home."

"You're probably right." Martika sighed. "But unfortunately, I wasn't so lucky."

"What do you mean?"

"I have *four* children," she continued. "But two of the pregnancies were terminated before they reached full term. And what I didn't understand until just recently is that the connection between siblings is very strong and cannot be severed by death—no matter how long each of them may have lived. Even if their existence is unknown to their siblings consciously, the deceased will attempt to make themselves known by any means necessary. I'm just so worried that I've done my living children a terrible disservice by keeping their siblings secret for so long."

Madisyn and I looked at each other in disbelief. I knew that some things were seldom talked about in polite society, but it seemed tragic that an experience of the magnitude of abortion was commonly hidden from close friends. I wasn't sure if she was overstating the metaphysical implications, but I knew that as a friend I wished I had known so I could have been more understanding and supportive.

"We didn't know."

"Nobody does." Martika wiped the tears from her eyes before continuing. "But I'm committed to doing something about it now. Some old friends of mine have just organized a meeting to help me."

"A meeting?" I asked. "Who are you going to meet with?"

"Not a 'meeting,'" Martika laughed. "A *meeting*. It's a powerful Native American ceremony that often involves coming together to help someone in need."

Madisyn and I glanced at each other and shrugged. I had never heard of a *meeting* before, although something about it intrigued me.

"Have you been before?" I asked.

"Oh yes—several times. But this will be the first time I've ever done so for myself. Truth be told, I'm actually quite nervous about it."

"What's it like?" I was getting more intrigued with every passing second.

"Hmm, that's a good question. The simple answer is that it's unlike anything else—it's definitely a unique experience. Let me see . . . it takes place in a tipi and usually begins around sunset and goes all night until morning—"

"Well, that counts me out," interrupted Madisyn. "If I don't get my eight hours, I'll be ruined for weeks. Why do all the best ceremonies happen at night?"

"I don't know." Martika laughed. "Throughout the night there are several regimented rituals that are accompanied by drumming and singing. Even the wood used in the fire must be prepared with a strict mindfulness of tradition."

I usually avoided organized Native American gatherings because most of the ones I had been exposed to previously had taken place in school gymnasiums or impersonal cultural centers. And although I wanted to deepen my relationship with my Indian ancestry, I felt uncomfortable doing so in such a modern context. However, hearing Martika talk about a tipi as the location of the meeting definitely got my attention.

"You're welcome to come if you'd like," Martika offered. "It would be lovely to have as many friendly faces as possible."

"That sounds great!" I was unquestionably excited, although I didn't want to leave Madisyn home alone. "Are you sure you don't want to come?" I asked her.

"There's no way I can stay up all night," Madisyn replied. "But you should definitely go. You need to connect with your heritage, and this is the first Native American event that you've been interested in since I've known you."

"You're probably right," I conceded. "Martika, when is it, and what should I bring?"

"It starts this Saturday night and goes through Sunday morning. You should bring some warm clothes, a blanket, and a cushion to sit on."

"You should also bring some water," Madisyn added.

"You can bring water," replied Martika, "but you'll need to leave it in your car. You'll be given water when you are *allowed* to drink. Like I said, the rituals are pretty rigid."

"I'm glad I'm not going." Madisyn scrunched up her face. "I don't like being told when I'm allowed to eat or drink. It reminds me of elementary school."

We all laughed, and Martika gave me directions to the ceremonial grounds and arranged a time for us to meet.

"Oh, I almost forgot," Martika said on her way out the door. "Be sure not to drink any alcohol between now and Saturday. Alcohol has a violent reaction to the *medicine,* and you'll get really sick if there's any in your system."

"Medicine?" I didn't have a problem abstaining from a glass of wine with dinner, but this was the first I'd heard about "medicine."

"Didn't I mention that? Oh, sorry. Yes, there will be sacred peyote medicine as part of this ceremony. You don't have to partake if you don't want to, but it is a significant part of the ritual."

"Peyote!" I exclaimed. "Are you serious? I thought that was illegal!"

"It is a controlled substance, but the N.A.C. has a religious exemption for use in ceremonies."

"What's the N.A.C.?" I felt like I was finding out about a secret society I'd never heard of before.

"Native American Church. It's actually the largest indigenous religion in the United States, although it wasn't formalized until the early 1900s. There are thousands of members all over the country, but they try to keep quiet because they don't want their rituals taken away from them."

My excitement about attending the ceremony was now greatly tempered with the knowledge that there would be psychedelic plants consumed during the ritual. I personally wasn't familiar with the effects of peyote, but everything I'd seen in movies and read in books portrayed it as a powerful drug that was difficult to control. There was no denying that I was drawn to everything Martika had shared, but I wasn't certain I was prepared to ingest a controlled substance.

"Wow, I don't know about that. I'm not sure I'm ready for peyote."

"You don't have to take it," Madisyn reiterated.

"But what's the point of going if I'm not going to participate fully? Isn't that a major part of the ceremony?"

"Yes, it is," said Martika. "But it *is* okay if you don't partake. Everybody is really nice, and there won't be any peer pressure if that's what you're worried about."

"I don't know . . ." I repeated. "I guess I just need to think about it."

"I totally understand—no pressure. Just tell me by Friday so I can make sure your place is reserved."

CHAPTER NINE

My anxiety about the *meeting* intensified appreciably during the rest of the week. I was sure there were many people who would be envious of the opportunity to experience peyote in a traditional ceremonial context, but I wasn't a big fan of mind-altering drugs and genuinely felt afraid of what might happen if I completely lost control. I had received most of my information about illicit substances from antidrug propaganda in elementary school, and although I was a big fan of psychedelic music from the 1960s, I personally wasn't drawn to the source of their inspiration.

As the weekend drew closer, I began to feel a knowing in my soul that it was something I *had* to do. It felt like a rite of passage and an ancestral doorway that I was compelled to pass through. And although I knew that my Cherokee lineage wasn't explicitly involved in the N.A.C., there was still something undeniably authentic about the *meeting* that resonated deep within my soul.

After I notified Martika that I was intending to attend, time accelerated at a blinding rate, as if to disallow second-guessing my decision. Once Saturday afternoon came around, I barely had time to gather all of my supplies so that I could arrive three hours early in order to ask the people in charge of the ceremony for permission to participate.

Thankfully, Martika was already there by the time I found the ceremonial grounds after winding over several unmarked dirt roads along the foothills of the Cascade Range. A massive muslin-hued tipi had been erected in a clearing among the conifer forest about a hundred yards from the road. The grounds were buzzing with activity as several groups of people feverishly prepared for the evening's occasion.

"Did you bring the pie?" Martika asked after greeting me with a hug. She'd been very explicit that I was to bring a marionberry pie as an offering when I asked permission to attend the ceremony. After scouring three different grocery stores, I eventually found the last pie in town.

"Yes, it's in the car."

"Good. Why don't you get it now, and we'll go to the house to meet the Road Man."

After retrieving the pie from my car, we walked up the dirt road toward a peeled red clapboard cabin at the end of the drive.

"What's a Road Man?" I asked.

"He's the person in charge of the *meeting*. Sort of like a priest in other religious traditions."

"Is he from this area?"

"No, he's from Arizona. He's constantly traveling across the country to perform various rituals. It's very important to honor him because of the many miles he travels to share his wisdom and ceremony."

"Is that why he's called a Road Man? Because he's on the road so much?"

"No." She laughed. "But that's a good thought. The reason he's called a Road Man is because he's the one who helps everyone navigate the Peyote Road. He has a very powerful connection to the spirit world and significant experience in handling the sacred medicine. You must surrender yourself to his care in order to journey on the Peyote Road. And when you ask permission, he will either grant or deny his assistance in doing so."

I began to get nervous about whether or not I would pass the test. In some ways I was hoping he would reject me so I wouldn't have to confront my fear of taking the peyote, but I also knew myself well enough to understand that my ego wouldn't let me give up without trying.

The inside of the house was bustling with activity as several women tended to three large iron pots boiling on the stove. The unusual aromas wafting from the cookware revealed a mélange of spices unlike any I had smelled before. Seated at the far end of the kitchen was a frail Indian man who was devouring a blood-rare slab of beef as if he hadn't eaten in weeks.

"Uncle Wayne!" Martika addressed the small man, and he returned the greeting with a toothless grin.

"Hello, niece," he mumbled through a mouthful of food before hastily returning his attention to the steak.

"When did you get in?"

"Morning," he grunted, without lifting his gaze from the plate of food.

"Are you doing okay?"

"Humph."

"Uncle Wayne," Martika continued, "I want to introduce you to a friend of mine. He's interested in attending the *meeting* tonight."

No response.

"His name is Scott." She gestured that I should introduce myself.

"Nice to meet you," I said as confidently as I could.

"He has Indian blood," Martika said.

No response.

"Cherokee," I interjected.

"Humph."

By this time I was concerned that I had already done something wrong to break protocol. I definitely wanted to attend the meeting, but more important was that I not offend someone I'd just met.

"I brought you a pie," I offered.

"What kind?" It was the first time the Road Man had addressed me, although he still wouldn't look in my direction.

"Marionberry."

"Humph." He gestured for me to put the pie on the table and then to sit in the empty chair across from him.

After I settled into the chair, he looked at me intensely with sunken, bloodshot eyes and mumbled, "Why you want to come to *meeting?*"

"Um . . ." I suddenly felt ill prepared and looked to Martika for support, but she was now by the stove chatting with the women making soup. I then closed my eyes and took a deep breath before the words came to me. "I want to support Martika . . . and I feel it's important to reconnect with my Indian heritage . . . to learn more about where I come from."

He continued to stare at me for several seconds and shifted his gaze, as if to study every pore on my face. I had never felt more self-conscious in all my life and surmised that even my soul was being judged by this wrinkled, toothless man.

"Medicine is teacher," he said after a long silence, straightening himself up before continuing. "I'm not teacher. Medicine is teacher. Understand?"

"Yes." I did my best to follow his garbled words, as he had resumed stuffing his mouth without the aid of a utensil.

"Medicine good. Alcohol bad. Drugs bad. Medicine help. Medicine puts us back on road. Red road."

I nodded intently.

"Medicine not drug. Medicine is teacher. Good teacher."

I continued to nod.

"Respect!" he yelled loudly and began pounding on his chest with his closed fist. "Medicine! Respect!"

The Road Man leaned toward me, and his nose nearly touched my own. His bloodshot eyes were open wide, and the fragile Indian man I had met moments before was long gone. He then whispered in an otherworldly voice that sent chills down my spine: *"Are you afraid of medicine?"*

I nodded slowly. "Yes, I am a bit afraid."

"Good." He leaned back and nodded understandingly. "Good to be afraid. But medicine is kind. Good teacher."

His attention turned back to the food before him as he placed an enormous wedge of marionberry pie on his dinner plate.

"Good pie," he mumbled while stuffing his mouth with the dessert. Large globs of indigo filling ran down his chin, and he wiped it clean with the back of his wrist.

Martika then returned to my side and put her hand on my shoulder to indicate we should leave. "Thank you, Uncle Wayne," she said as she guided me out of the kitchen.

As we exited the front door, I heard him grunt one last time. "Humph."

"He seemed to like you," Martika said as we walked back toward the tipi grounds.

"Really?" I laughed. "Are you sure? It didn't seem that way to me!"

"Definitely. He usually doesn't say more than two words to someone he's just met. He's really nice when you get to know him, but he's understandably wary of the motivations of new people."

"I suppose that makes sense. There are probably a lot of people who just want access to peyote."

"More than you know. Scott, I need to return home for a few hours to prepare for the *meeting.* I suggest you stay here and see if you can help out.

The *meeting* is going to be really full tonight, and you might lose your place in line if you leave."

"I can stay." After the conversation with Uncle Wayne, I felt it was probably best to remain so I wouldn't lose my nerve. "What should I do to help?"

"The tall man near the tipi owns this property—he'd be a good person to ask. His name is Stefan."

Stefan was occupied with stacking long sections of carefully prepared logs near the entrance of the tipi. Each one was between three and four feet in length and had been completely stripped of its bark, as well as any branches or imperfections.

After I introduced myself, Stefan asked me to fold the blankets covering the sweat lodge and stack them inside the plywood shed nearby.

I had never seen a sweat lodge up close before, and the dome-like structure was much smaller than I would have expected. It was no more than five feet tall and ten feet in diameter and was topped with a dozen gray padded moving blankets. I was amazed to discover the skeleton of thin willow branches under the blankets that was responsible for sustaining their considerable weight. Once the coverings had been completely put away,

I admired the shallow pit inside the structure, which was filled with stacks of porous lava rocks.

Martika had invited me to attend the sweat-lodge ceremony the night before, but seeing how small the austere lodge was made me glad that I'd decided to wait. *One thing at a time,* I thought.

After Stefan told me there was nothing left to do, I relaxed on a nearby picnic bench as the sun retreated behind the rocky Cascades. Before long, a well-dressed Indian man joined me and began pulling out several items from a green canvas duffel bag. He wore a long-sleeved button-down shirt, a black leather vest, and a braided bolo tie that was cinched with a polished silver-and-turquoise clasp.

He started by removing a red silk sheath from a small cast-iron cooking pot. It was no more than eight inches high and slightly wider in diameter. He reverently placed the kettle on the table and carefully removed various objects from inside. The first was a well-worn folded leather disk cut about twice the diameter of the kettle. He then retrieved seven perfectly round black stones, an ebony-colored carved wooden stick, and a generous length of white cord.

When the kettle had been completely emptied of its contents, the man held his palms over the objects and began to recite a prayer in his native language. I felt as if I were imposing by staring at him during this obviously intimate moment, but I couldn't take my eyes off him or stop listening to his gravelly voice. Although I couldn't understand what he was saying, his words captured my very soul and held it firmly until he finished.

Once his devotion was complete, he retrieved a canteen from his bag and began to speak in English. Although he wasn't looking at me, I was aware that his words were for my benefit.

> *"Many years ago, my great-great-grandfather had everything stolen from him. His land. His drum. His family."*

He emptied his canteen full of water into the iron kettle.

> *"But the music in his heart kept beating even after everything was gone. When he was sent to the reservation, he was told to never strike the drum again or else he would be killed, like his father and his uncles had been. But the drum kept beating in his heart."*

He then submerged the leather disk into the kettle and began massaging it underwater.

> *"Periodically those who had stolen would invite themselves into his home on the reservation. They would pretend to be his friend, but he knew the real reason they visited. They were looking for the drum. The drum was very powerful. They were afraid of the drum."*

He removed the leather and wrung it out like a used washcloth. The hide had become supple in the water, and he placed it over the mouth of the kettle.

> *"In the surrounding forests at night, his family would gather to meet and receive medicine. But the medicine needed the drum. The drum is the heartbeat of the medicine."*

Retrieving one of the marble-like stones, he placed it under the leather on the side of the kettle and then wrapped cord around it so that its shape protruded through the leather.

"So he made a new drum from the iron kettle that had been given to him by his captors to cook his food."

The wrapping continued until the cord had been woven around each of the seven stones and secured at the bottom of the kettle. Within minutes the ordinary cooking utensil had transformed into a beautifully crafted drum that would have been at home in a museum.

"It was a good drum. A powerful drum. He would carry it to the forest at night to bring the heartbeat back. The medicine was happy."

He struck the drum with the hand-carved ebony stick, which filled the air with a thunderous sound. It was extraordinary how loud the small drum was, and it resonated as if it were several times larger.

"And when the ceremony was over, he would untie the drum and return the kettle to his kitchen alongside the plates and utensils he had been given."

After striking the drum several times in succession, he brought it to his mouth and bit into the skin of the drum, tipping it forward as if he were drinking soup. When he returned it to the table, a small puddle of water had pooled from the punctures left by his teeth. He spread the liquid around the surface of the drum skin before tightening the cord and striking it again. The drum was repeatedly tuned in this way until it satisfied the master craftsman.

Martika joined us as soon as the drum maker was finished. She had changed her clothes and was wearing a long maroon loose-fitting dress with delicate yellow birds embroidered around the bodice.

"I see you met Keyan," she said. "He comes from a long history of Drum Men."

"Yes, he was telling me," I replied, giving her a hug.

"Hello, Martika," Keyan greeted my friend as he stood up. "Tonight is your *meeting.* I have come from South Dakota and will provide the heartbeat for your medicine."

"Thank you for coming all the way here. When Uncle Wayne asked me who I wanted to drum, I could only think of you. I'm very happy you were able to join us."

"My pleasure."

"It's almost dark." Martika turned to me. "I have to go in now, but I'll save you a spot next to me."

I nodded as she disappeared through the womblike opening of the tipi, which revealed a fire burning inside. The glow of the flames stood in warm contrast to the indigo twilight that had descended on the mountainous landscape surrounding the ceremonial grounds.

Suddenly, nearly everyone who had arrived gathered near me in front of the tipi. The crowd was unusually quiet, and although a few acknowledged me with a simple nod, most were obviously concentrating on their own experience and preparing themselves for the night ahead.

My anxiety returned, and I once again felt nervous about what might happen during the ceremony. In that moment I became aware that it was more than just the peyote that intimidated me. Whatever was inside the tipi would change my life forever, and I knew that I would never be the same.

CHAPTER TEN

Thankfully, Martika saved me a place, because by the time I followed the eager crowd into the tipi, most of the available spots inside had already been taken. We were directed to walk around the fire clockwise, and fortunately, I remembered Martika's warning to always face the flames while I was inside. It sounded easier than it was, and I nearly fell over trying to sit down without turning my back to the fire. I never realized how natural it was to turn around before sitting cross-legged on the floor.

Once I was situated, I could appreciate the simple beauty of how the inside of the tipi had been prepared. Closest to the opening were ten wooden poles intricately layered on top of one another to form an arrowlike structure. Impressive flames burned brightly where the tips of these poles crossed, filling the center of the tipi with flickering light.

Surrounding the fire at the opposite end of the tipi was a narrow shelf that had been meticulously sculpted from the soil into the shape of a massive elliptical half circle. It was no more than two inches above the ground, but the craftsmanship was remarkable, as evinced by the flawlessly level surface.

"What is that?" I whispered to Martika, pointing toward the peculiar dirt sculpture.

"That is *The Moon*—the altar that houses Father Peyote."

As she mentioned this, I noticed a dark brown peyote button planted near the center of the altar. It seemed to emanate waves of unseen energy, and I felt its power in the pit of my stomach whenever I stared directly at it—my nervousness was compounded greatly in its presence.

"Is that what we're going to eat?"

"No," she whispered. "That one is not for us. Father Peyote is a sacred talisman that belongs to the Road Man. It is not to be eaten and is the source of much of the Road Man's power."

I recognized Uncle Wayne sitting cross-legged behind The Moon, elevated by three large pillows. Immediately in front of him was a small red cloth upon which several feathers, small boxes, and animal bones were crowded. To his left, Keyan was also sitting on large pillows, with his reconstructed water drum resting between his crossed legs. To the Road Man's right was an elderly Indian gentleman, also resting on large pillows. He appeared the most preoccupied of the three and seemed to be looking at the fire and within himself simultaneously.

"Who's that?" I whispered.

"The Cedar Man."

Uncle Wayne nodded to the man tending the fire at the opposite end of the tipi. Without a sound, the man deftly untied the flap of the tipi opening and it quickly fell shut. Immediately, all whispers hushed and everyone fell to silence, turning their attention to Father Peyote. The small button appeared to have grown to nearly twice its previous size, and the energy emanating from it forced me backward. I felt the back of my head brush against the wall of the tipi.

The muscular man tending the flames picked up a handmade broom and began sweeping the ground between the fire pit and everyone seated around the tipi. Within just a few minutes, the dirt was meticulously groomed, and all our footprints had been brushed into a crisscross pattern that reminded me of a Zen rock garden.

The Cedar Man then approached the fire and dipped his fingers into a yellow buckskin pouch adorned with an intricately beaded bird. Removing his hand from the bag, he flung a handful of its contents into the fire, which crackled and sent a generous plume of smoke toward the peak of the tipi. He fed three additional handfuls to the flames, and the air filled with the unmistakable musky scent of cedar. I found the distinctive aroma to be rather comforting, as it reminded me of chopping wood when I was a child.

"Bless yourself with cedar," the Road Man commanded as he held his palms toward the fire. The people around me followed his lead and confidently scooped the elusive plumes of smoke and "bathed" themselves with it. Starting from the top of their heads and progressing down to their feet, everyone looked like they were blissfully showering in the most luxurious oils on Earth. I attempted to do the same, but I felt awkward trying to catch the smoke and direct it where I wanted it to go.

Uncle Wayne then retrieved a stack of rectangular yellow sheets from the miscellany in front of him, and after taking one for himself, passed the rest on to Keyan. He licked the sheet, systematically covering every inch with saliva. When the bundle reached me, I encountered dozens of carefully flattened corn husks that had been trimmed to exactly the same size—approximately four inches by three inches. I followed everyone else's lead and put the tasteless sheet in my mouth, passing the rest onward.

While I busily moistened the ridged husk, Uncle Wayne retrieved a small leather pouch and extracted a generous pinch of tobacco before passing it along. He expertly rolled the husk into a near perfect cylinder and held it together by licking its edges.

I attempted to mimic the master roller, but mine ended up looking less like a cigarette and more like a thin, lumpy burrito with shredded tobacco twigs limply hanging out the ends. I tried to seal it shut by licking the edges, but the husk defiantly refused to cooperate.

Meanwhile, the Fire Man tended to an eighteen-inch wooden cylinder whose pointed end was smoldering deep within the center blaze. He carefully rotated it as if he were turning a rotisserie, and would remove it periodically to blow on the tip until it glowed bright red. He repeated this process as the tobacco pouch made its way to everyone in the tipi before Uncle Wayne returned it to its place.

With a nod, the Road Man summoned the glowing wooden cylinder, and the Fire Man presented it with ceremonial reverence. Uncle Wayne blew on the pointed tip so that the crackling embers glowed brightly, and then used it to ignite one edge of his corn-husk cigarette while he eagerly puffed. The large wooden lighter looked grossly out of scale in comparison to the relatively small cigarette, but there was something gracefully majestic about the way the coals coaxed smoke from the rolled corn husk.

By the time the lighter was passed to me, the embers had retreated deep inside. My lung capacity was challenged as I attempted to revive the burning coals with my inhalation. It took several tries before the corn husk began to smolder, and I accidentally breathed the smoke into my lungs during the process, coughing uncomfortably for several seconds.

Once everyone in the tipi had successfully ignited their tobacco, the Road Man got our attention with a gravelly whisper:

"Tonight we meet for Martika. Her family. Her children. Her children who are here. Her children who are gone."

He held the corn-husk cigarette with his thumb and forefinger and deliberately brought it to his lips, inhaling deeply. As he exhaled, a river of smoke left his lips and floated above all of us like a giant halo.

"And we pray," he continued. "We pray for Martika. For her children. For our family. For ourselves . . ." He drew another breath from the tobacco and lifted his head and blew a thin stream of smoke toward the peak of the tipi. ". . . Father Sky . . ." Returning his gaze to level, he exhaled a sea of smoke that gradually kissed the forehead of each of the people gathered around the fire. He then looked to the ground and blew a needle of smoke that lingered when it reached the dirt. ". . . Mother Earth."

Uncle Wayne closed his eyes and began to mumble in his native tongue as a chorus of voices joined in. Everyone in the tipi vocalized their prayers while puffing on their smoldering corn husks. At first I could hear the distinct crackling of burning tobacco, lifting the prayers to the sky, yet within seconds the voices had filled the air and I could no longer even hear my own breath.

It felt oddly voyeuristic to eavesdrop on so many people at once, although it was genuinely touching to hear them outwardly express their heartfelt love and concern without a trace of self-consciousness. Because everyone was speaking at the same time, I couldn't distinguish any single prayer, although I was able to discern a few words that were regularly repeated: "Martika . . . children . . . love . . . hope . . . medicine . . ."

The prayers continued to escalate in volume and intensity until the energy had begun to swirl inside the tipi, as strong as a summer breeze before a storm. The magical way the words took on a life of their own sent chills up and down my spine.

I brought the corn husk to my lips and followed the lead of those around me by exhaling once to the sky, once facing forward, and once to the ground directly in front of me. At first my insecurity nearly prevented the words from escaping my lips, but when I noticed that my individual voice was hungrily swallowed up by the prayer ocean cresting around me, for the first time in my life I was able to confidently express myself in prayer.

"Please give Martika the strength to heal her past, and kindly support each of her children with love and forgiveness for their mother."

Soon the energy in the room began to shift dramatically. Whereas at first the prayers were all swirling together with a single purpose, the intentions quickly diverged, and the sound and energy metamorphosed into something decidedly more dissonant. The decibel level jumped several points, and I found it almost impossible to tolerate the roar of so many people all praying at the top of their lungs.

I strained to eavesdrop through the cacophony and discovered that Martika was no longer the singular subject of the prayers—everyone had begun to pray for themselves and their families. It was as if the prayers for Martika were almost a polite overture, and once everyone began to pray for themselves, the tone became much more desperate and insistent.

My thoughts turned to Madisyn and the difficulties she'd had with the pregnancy. I still hadn't recovered from witnessing how physically violent the miscarriage had been, let alone dealt with the emotional and spiritual wounds inflicted by Autumn when she didn't follow through with the pregnancy.

I closed my eyes tightly and concentrated on my love for Madisyn before my next prayer commenced.

"Please be with my wife during the next few months and give her the confidence to get pregnant again. Give her the strength to conceive a healthy baby and the stamina to support it through a full term. I understand that the miscarriage was perfect in the divine plan of the universe, but I humbly ask for compassion to allow us to be able to bring our baby into the world without any further complications.

"For Autumn . . . I pray for you. For your ability to feel safe and wanted, and to come through your mother, Madisyn, into this world so we can all be together as a family. We love you dearly and don't blame you for anything that happened before. I apologize that you have had to wait so long for us to prepare for your arrival. We've had many experiences in this lifetime that have made us better people, and we are ready for you now. We have no doubts, and I promise you will be cared for deeply.

You are our daughter, and we will love you forever."

It was difficult to pray for Autumn, but once I did so, a burden that I had been unaware I was carrying was released. A deep sadness had lodged itself within the back of my throat during the miscarriage, and the prayer had exposed it by allowing it to finally be felt. It wasn't completely gone, but by acknowledging the wound I'd been oblivious to, I sensed that healing was finally able to commence.

"And for myself, I pray that this ceremony will connect me with my heritage and give me a purpose and sense of being within my family line. I pray that the medicine will be kind and teach me what I need to know to be a better person and to prepare myself for the journey of fatherhood."

The voices in the tipi slowly began to fade as everyone finished their prayers. A collective sense of relief filled the tipi, and everyone seemed several years younger after their burdens had been lifted. It was as if we had all taken a psychic bath and were now thoroughly clean and refreshed.

After the last person had finished praying, we sat in silence for several minutes without moving. There was a palpable sense of release that accompanied the silence, and I felt my entire body relax, after being able to hear my own breath again.

Out of the corner of my eye I noticed Keyan beginning to stir, and when I turned my gaze toward him, I could see that he had placed his drum on the ground between his crossed legs. He then passed a handmade rattle to Uncle Wayne and watched intently as the Road Man turned it in his hands to carefully examine the gourd attached to the hand-carved wooden handle.

All eyes were fixed on the rattle, and everyone collectively held their breath while he waved it over Father Peyote as if it were a magic wand. The feathers hanging from the rattle softly kissed the sacred button, and once the Road Man seemed satisfied that the rattle and the cactus had been properly introduced, he sat upright and began to shake the instrument intently.

Schk, schk, schk, schk, schk, schk, schk . . .

The rattle punctuated the silence with an insistent rhythm that commanded our full attention. The Road Man shook it with little variation for nearly a minute before Keyan joined in with the water drum I had watched him reconstruct outside.

Puhm, puhm, puhm, puhm, puhm, puhm, puhm . . .

The drum's rhythm was nearly identical to the rattle's, although with its more forceful tone, I could feel it deep within my core, and my own heartbeat gradually sped up to keep time.

Uncle Wayne began to sing with a gravelly voice that had more in common with Delta blues vocalists than the traditional Native American musicians I'd been exposed to previously. The soulful melody floated over the top of the repetitive percussion in a way that seemed almost disconnected from the supporting beats. I'd never heard music sung with such unusual intonation before, and at first I found it quite difficult to follow.

The Road Man kept repeating the lyrics until he ended up satisfying some internal rule that wasn't obvious to me. Once the rattle ceased to shake, Keyan quickly tipped the drum on its side and struck the stretched skin with his hand-carved stick. As the water inside the drum sloshed, the pitch slid around in a manner more akin to a trombone than a percussive instrument.

The Road Man handed the rattle to Stefan, who was sitting on the opposite side of Keyan. He held the rattle still with both hands in a prayer position, and then without warning began to shake it with a fervor similar to that exhibited by Uncle

Wayne. Within moments, he too began to sing, although his voice didn't have the same intensity. Once the first verse had concluded, nearly every person in the tipi confidently chorused the second even though it was in a language that didn't resemble any I was familiar with.

The rattle continued to be passed from one person to the next, each of whom took the liberty of leading the entire tipi in song. Thankfully, Martika handed it over without singing, which made it easier for me to do the same. I wanted to take the time to examine the rattle's artistic beauty, but I was afraid that Keyan would begin drumming and everyone would wait for me to sing. Therefore, the rattle remained in my hands for no longer than a few seconds before I carefully presented it to the person on my left.

As more songs were performed, I started to feel comfortable joining the chorus to echo the lyrics as best I could. The unusual songs began to sound much more natural, and after a while my ears opened up and I was able to fully appreciate the music's perfect beauty. I then surrendered to the spirit of the ancient sounds, which gracefully prepared me for whatever would happen next.

Once the rattle had completed its first journey around the circumference of the tipi, the Road Man gently placed it on the ground next to a small wooden box, which he'd been blessing with an eagle feather. After waving the feather above the box one last time, he unhinged the top and removed a small clay pot and cradled it in his hand. He then retrieved a generous pinch of the container's mysterious contents and placed it in his mouth.

"That's the medicine," whispered Martika. "It's been dried and shredded."

I nodded, and watched him take a second and third helping before passing the ceramic vessel on to Keyan. He, too, consumed three portions and passed it to his left before bringing his drum into position.

The percussion resumed, and the Road Man once again led the group in song. However, instead of looking at the attendees while singing, he concentrated on Father Peyote and serenaded the small cactus button with all his might.

I wasn't able to take my eyes off of the clay pot as it gradually made its way around the tipi, each person reverently consuming between one and three generous helpings of the shredded peyote.

By the time it was only three people away from me, I was beside myself with apprehension and felt like I'd made a grave mistake in attending.

Martika noticed my panic attack and held my hand gently while smiling supportively.

"You can pass the medicine if you want," she whispered. "You don't need to have any."

I nodded, considering her words. She was right. There was nothing wrong with *not* taking the peyote. I would still benefit from the prayers and rituals of the ceremony.

Soon the clay pot was in Martika's hands. I watched carefully as she took a minuscule pinch of the tealike medicine. She swallowed hard, making it obvious that she didn't like the taste at all. Bowing her head, she then ceremoniously handed me the red ceramic dish with both hands.

My nervousness evaporated once the vessel of shredded peyote was in my hands. I was immediately calmed by it, and I held it for several seconds while deciding what to do. Just as I was about to pass the clay pot onward, I heard a familiar voice echo in my head.

You are here for the medicine.

It took me a moment to register who was speaking. I recognized the voice of my Cherokee great-grandfather, who had helped guide me through many adventures during my spiritual awakening. I knew that if he was with me, I could handle anything.

With my actions entirely disconnected from my conscious mind, I watched myself dip my thumb and forefinger into the clay pot and remove a small pinch of peyote. I brought it to my mouth and let it fall onto my tongue. It had a grainy consistency and a distinctive taste that could only be described as *salty ash*. Surprisingly, it didn't repulse me, as it had seemed to do Martika; and while I was chewing, I discovered that I unexpectedly enjoyed its intense, musty flavor. Something about it was unusual and intriguing. But the thing that was most remarkable was the indescribable feeling of familiarity that the grainy cactus elicited. There was something deep in my soul's memory that was very familiar with the taste in my mouth.

I passed the clay pot to the person on my left and patiently waited for the effects of the peyote to overtake me. I didn't know exactly what to expect, but I guessed it would be similar to the feeling I'd had in the past when my soul had left my body to visit the spirit world. I purposely didn't research the effects before attending the meeting because I didn't want to have any preconceived notions that might influence the experience.

By the time the medicine vessel had returned to Uncle Wayne, I still wasn't feeling any sensation that could qualify as resulting directly from the peyote. Looking around, it seemed that many people were starting to feel the effects, as evinced by closed eyes and swaying torsos. I didn't know how long it was supposed to take, and the only way I was able to mark the passage of time was when another person took the rattle and commenced singing from the voluminous peyote songbook.

I decided to close my eyes and see if I could coax the desired effect by concentrating on disconnecting my soul from my body. It was a skill I had learned at a very young age and could usually summon up quite easily. However, at that moment it was nearly impossible to disconnect, as it felt like a force would pull me back into my body every time I tried to float away. I had never experienced so much resistance before, and began to get frustrated. I concluded that I probably hadn't taken enough peyote, and I finally decided to wait patiently for everyone else's experience to end.

When I opened my eyes, I was disappointed to find that nothing had changed. I wasn't having an otherworldly experience—in fact, quite the opposite. In that moment, the ground seemed so obviously mundane that even the ceremonial preparations could no longer cover up the undeniable fact that we were sitting on nothing more than garden-variety *dirt.* I began to feel sorry for the people surrounding me who were all buying into this sham of a spiritual practice. I'd been exposed to profound metaphysical experiences many times before, and this appeared to be no more than a group of well-intentioned lemmings thinking good thoughts while ingesting mind-altering substances. Perhaps the ceremony had first originated from a genuine tradition, but on this night it felt no more profound than watching a Saturday-morning cartoon.

Then a plaintive voice with a thick Native American accent emerged from the incessant drumming and spoke to me directly.

You are one of them.

For some reason these words annoyed me, and I quickly turned around to confront the person who had spoken them. My nose nearly made contact with the canvas wall—clearly there was no room for anyone behind me. I looked in vain for where the voice might have come from and discovered that nobody had moved an inch. Once I realized that the sound wasn't corporeal in origin, I assumed it must have come from my great-grandfather. But when it spoke again, I realized that the voice was entirely unfamiliar.

You must remain on the soil.

Without skipping a beat, I found myself urgently explaining to the voice in my head why I intended to commune with the spirit world. I told him that one of my gifts was to be able to travel to other worlds and that I needed to speak with my unborn daughter to make her feel comfortable about making the journey to this planet. And that I was hoping that the medicine would help me be with her.

I am helping.

How do you expect your child to feel at peace with this earth if you can't remain here yourself? Children look to their parents for guidance and support by watching their actions. If you want your child to come into this world, you must remain here yourself.

You must remain on the soil.

These wise words profoundly humbled me, and I felt ashamed that I had doubted the integrity of the ceremony. The medicine was right. If I wanted

Autumn to be born on this planet, I needed to invite her to where *I* was living.

It was time to begin acting like a parent, not a friend.

Suddenly the music stopped, and I couldn't help feeling that someone was looking at me. When I turned to my right, I found Martika staring at me intently.

"Are you okay?" she asked.

"Uh-huh." I didn't know how to begin to explain what had just happened, but it was comforting to see her smile.

"It's almost midnight—they just brought in the water. Are you thirsty?"

I nodded, realizing that I was indeed dehydrated. I had a severe case of peyote mouth, and my saliva had formed a gummy mush that made it difficult to swallow.

She handed me a galvanized pail, which sloshed with water as I placed it between my crossed legs. I dipped the stainless-steel ladle into the bucket and brought it to my lips, careful not to spill any on myself. The first mouthful of ice-cold water evaporated on contact with my sandpaper tongue. After the third drink, the water finally made it to the back of my throat and all the way down to my stomach. I eventually forced myself to stop drinking, after noticing there wasn't much water left for the rest of the people in the tipi.

After everyone had rehydrated themselves with the modest ration of water, the drumming resumed in force, as did another round of passionate chanting. Although I couldn't be certain, I still wasn't able to pick out a repeated song, and I was impressed with the sheer volume of lyrics that nearly everyone seemed to know by heart.

By the time the second round of peyote was circulating, my left leg had fallen hopelessly asleep. I was used to being in bed by midnight, and evidently my leg hadn't received the memo that we were staying up all night. After helping myself to a much larger pinch of the salty ash than the first time, I slowly began to massage my leg back into consciousness. My foot was the first to stir, but it wasn't pleased to be interrupted from its slumber. It punished me by stabbing my arch with hundreds of imaginary needles that felt excruciatingly painful with the slightest movement.

Thankfully, I was able to coax my leg back to normal by sitting "sidesaddle" while once again waiting for the medicine to take effect.

I repeatedly found myself staring into the fire and watching as the flames danced to the rhythm of the water drum. The fire surged and fell with the beat, and periodically contributed its own voice by crackling precisely in time with the music.

When Uncle Wayne began to lead us in song again, he shook the rattle with such intensity that I thought the head of the shaker would fly off. Veins protruded from his neck, and his eyes were fixed intently on the fire in the center of the tipi. There was also a tone of desperation and urgency in his voice that was frighteningly intense. It was almost as if he were trying to summon the very soul of the fire to reveal itself and walk among us.

As I returned my gaze to the fire, it appeared as if he'd been successful in enticing it to burn with much more of a frenzy than it had before. The flames licked the air with such determination that I wondered if they would reach the sloping walls of the tipi and ignite our shelter.

Then I saw the first one.

A misty figure emerged from the flames and floated briefly above the blaze before disappearing into the air. It was vaguely human in form, yet it resembled an infant more than a grown adult. At first I thought I had imagined it, but as I continued to gaze into the embers, another figure emerged and again floated a few feet from the fire before fading away.

The Road Man continued his intense engagement, and the more I watched, the more it seemed obvious that he was the one responsible for extracting the spirits from the flames. Every time a new one would reveal itself, he would flinch slightly and gesture with his free hand in the direction of the ethereal shapes.

After a while several of the spirits had still not disappeared, and instead remained inside the tipi, hovering in the space above our heads and curling into the fetal position, as if the tipi had transformed into a giant uterus. They kept emerging from the fire until there were at least two or three spirits for each corporeal attendee. Before long the tipi was filled with all the spirit babies that had arrived.

As I looked around, it seemed as if everyone besides me and Uncle Wayne were oblivious to our guests.

Suddenly, the Road Man stopped singing and rested the rattle on the ground in front of him. He gazed up at the floating "nursery" and then stared intensely into Martika's eyes before speaking.

"My niece Martika brought four babies into this world."

Martika gulped nervously.

"But only two remain here. Her two other children were taken by her own hand. They call it abortion. But the babies don't understand. The babies are confused. So the babies *haunt* their brother and sister. The brother and sister have difficult lives. Because they live for the babies who cannot live for themselves."

His harsh words shocked me.

I had always felt that a woman should be able to make any choice regarding her own body, and it was disconcerting to be confronted with the assertion that a baby's soul might not understand what happened as a result of such a difficult decision. This realization reinforced my belief that medical care needed to get better at taking a holistic view of healing in order to treat not only the body, but the soul as well. In some ways it seemed like the indigenous cultures were substantially ahead of Western medicine in this regard, and it was fascinating to witness firsthand.

"Tonight we release the two babies," Uncle Wayne continued. "They travel back to spirit world.

They belong in spirit world. Let brother and sister live here in peace."

The Road Man uttered a barely audible prayer under his breath while rolling a large ball of peyote between his palms. He then placed the medicine in his mouth and swallowed it whole without flinching. He continued to pray as he rolled a slightly smaller-sized ball for Martika. When it was passed to my friend, she stared at it suspiciously for several seconds before taking a small bite out of it, as if it were a miniature apple. It took her three tiny bites to finish the brownish ball of dried cactus, and when she was done, she thirstily downed the small jar of water that was handed to her.

"Martika," Uncle Wayne spoke again, "you explain to first baby why you didn't want baby here."

I heard a gasp from nearly everyone in the tipi, and I stared at Uncle Wayne in disbelief. I was shocked by what he was asking my friend to do.

As Martika collected her thoughts, one of the spirit babies floated down from above and hovered between the fire and its mother. I was surprised that no one seemed to see the baby, although I received a pointed gesture of acknowledgment from Uncle Wayne when he noticed that I was also aware of our guests.

"You were my second child," Martika said in the direction of the spirit hovering in front of her. "I was very young when I found out I was pregnant with you—I was only seventeen years old. I was overwhelmed with taking care of my first child, and when I found out I was pregnant again . . ."

Martika's voice cracked, and she attempted to wipe away tears with the back of her hand before continuing.

"When I found out I was pregnant again," she repeated softly, "I left my baby and my husband—I ran away from both of them. And when I was gone . . . I just couldn't bear the thought of caring for another child . . ."

She broke down sobbing and bent over so her forehead rested on the ground, her body shuddering with every whimper. It was painful to watch the agony my friend was going through, although I had a strong feeling it was inappropriate to comfort her at that moment—she had to deal with this alone. After a long, emotional cry, Martika sat back up and looked directly at the spirit baby, who was still hovering in front of the fire.

". . . so I made them take you away from me—from my body. And you were gone. Gone forever."

Martika took a deep breath before continuing.

"I'm sorry I didn't want you. I wasn't strong enough to be your mother. Anybody's mother. I just couldn't do it. I hurt you deeply, and I'm eternally sorry. I just couldn't be your mother . . ."

Her words trailed off, and still shaking, she turned to Uncle Wayne. Even as the fire continued to roar, there was a palpable chill in the air that blew over us all.

Uncle Wayne nodded and began to speak directly to the first spirit baby, who was now looking in the Road Man's direction.

"It is time for you to go. You go to spirit world now. That is your home."

He began to chant in his native tongue and gesticulated dramatically in the direction of the spirit baby. He continued praying for several minutes before picking up a narrow white tubular object from among the ceremonial items laid out in front of him. He brought the slender animal bone to his lips and blew, coaxing out a high-pitched whistle.

The spirit baby visibly shuddered and appeared to be sucked toward the fire with every note. Suddenly the essence connected with the raging fire and shot up the flames and out the top of the tipi. As soon as it was gone, the Cedar Man rushed over with his beaded pouch and threw a generous handful of dried cedar into the fire. The needles smoked and crackled, seemingly ushering the baby's spirit to the next world.

Uncle Wayne nodded approvingly at the Cedar Man before returning his gaze to Martika.

"Continue," he said to her confidently.

Without warning a second spirit baby descended from above and floated into position, patiently waiting for its mother to speak.

"You were my third child," Martika continued, letting out an exhausted sigh. "I became pregnant with you while your father was still married to someone else. I didn't want you because I wasn't sure if he and I would be together. I didn't want to further complicate the relationship."

Martika's sobs continued as everyone's eyes were glued to her.

"We married the following year and remained together for seventeen years. But I never told your father about you—I thought he would leave me if he found out."

The second spirit baby began to spin around in place, faster and faster.

"I'm sorry. You have every right to be angry with me. But yesterday I mailed him a letter and told him everything. He will know soon."

The baby slowly came to a halt, and its gaze softened. I felt a connection open between the infant and its mother, and a sense of peace filled the tipi.

"I will always love you as my third child. You are worthy of my love, and I will never again hide you from anyone."

Martika pressed her fists firmly to her eyes for several seconds before continuing. She turned to Uncle Wayne and uttered two words:

"That's it."

Without missing a beat, Uncle Wayne retrieved the bone whistle and began to speak to the floating infant.

"It is time for you to go. You go to spirit world now. That is your home."

The Road Man repeated his chants and passionately blew the whistle, and the Cedar Man returned to the fire and sprinkled a generous handful of needles, which filled the tipi with smoke. The baby followed the path of its sibling and floated into the flames and out the tipi's peak to its new home.

With his free hand, Uncle Wayne retrieved the rattle and once again accompanied Keyan in the percussive duet they had begun hours before. The drumbeat was precise and insistent, while the rattle sounded more emphatic and purposeful than it had before. Periodically, the bone whistle sounded; and when its piercing, shrill notes reached our ears, another spirit baby would descend from the floating nursery above us. It would then connect with the fire at the precise moment that another handful of cedar was cast onto the flames, crackling and smoking, propelling the infant soul up and out of the tipi.

Drum. Rattle. Drum. Rattle. Drum. Rattle. Rattle.

The ensemble repeated its refrain as the fire rose higher and higher toward the sky, licking the air inside the canvas walls of the tipi with its scorching orange tongue.

Whistle. Whistle. Crackle. Roar.

By the time the last baby departed, I was physically and emotionally exhausted. I was in awe of the raw stamina Uncle Wayne had displayed during the relentless refrain, but I no longer had the energy to remain fully present.

The ceremony lasted for several hours longer, and I essentially checked out mentally and spent the rest of the night staring out the peak of the tipi where the babies had exited. I watched for hours as the pinhole constellations revealed the next world, where the children would finally be able to live in peace.

Seasons turn,
the snow is water again.

Rivers will flow.

CHAPTER ELEVEN

Summer came quickly that year, and our lives had nearly returned to normal by the time of the solstice. Ashland was always a beautiful town, but the warmest season of the year attracted hordes of tourists to the Shakespearean theaters, spurring a flurry of activity on par with a city five times its size. Many locals avoided the downtown area during the summer for that very reason, but I would often enjoy the surge of energy the visitors brought with them.

Madisyn and I were outside as often as possible and made a point of visiting the many hidden gems showcasing Ashland's natural beauty. Our favorite place was the Fairy Ponds at the edge of town, and we spent as much free time as we could exploring, and soaking in its charms. One of the most magical settings in all of Ashland, it felt like a medieval forest shrouded by natural arbors of hundred-year-old trees stretching majestically along the creek. A suite of shallow ponds gave the water a place to rest before rushing across the smoothed rocks and fallen branches along the meandering waterway. "Did you see *her* in the tipi?" Madisyn asked one day after perching on a favorite boulder adjacent to one of the smaller ponds.

"No." I knew when she was talking about Autumn because of the way she always arched her left eyebrow in the shape of a bassinet. "But I had an epiphany about how to remain present, and supportive of her transition."

"What was that?"

"It's hard to describe, but it boils down to acting more like a father and less like a friend."

"I think that's an ongoing challenge of being a parent." She smiled.

"Probably." I picked up a twig and tossed it upstream. We both watched as it deftly navigated around the maze of rocks before gracefully floating out of sight. "Sometimes I wonder if there's any point in having the ability to communicate with spirits in other dimensions."

"I know." She laughed. "Why can't they just leave us alone?"

Although Madisyn's psychic gifts were much different from my own, she was also burdened by supernatural communication. I was sure I would have gone crazy if my life partner hadn't been able to relate to what I was going through.

"Exactly," I agreed. "It would be much easier if the only voices we heard were those of the people physically in the room with us."

She nodded sympathetically.

"It's hard enough to learn how we're supposed to act in the world with all the different types of people on this planet. Everyone has different wants and needs, and it's so easy to say or do the wrong thing even in the best of situations. But when you have to balance that with the expectations of disincarnate souls, it's almost impossible to make everyone happy."

"Wouldn't it be great if we were born with instruction manuals?" Madisyn asked rhetorically. "Something that would explain all the rules about how we're supposed to live."

"That sounds like a good idea—maybe you should write one."

"Maybe I will." She smiled. "But at least we're lucky we weren't raised in families whose religious beliefs would demonize us or make us feel bad about our gifts."

"That's true—that would be horrible. But are psychic gifts really that special, or is everyone born with them? I mean, don't we all have the ability to tune in to other dimensions if we simply nurture it?"

Madisyn shrugged. "Probably."

"Because it seems like everyone has had at least one experience in life when they've felt some sort of communication from the other side."

"Like when you think about a friend right before they call—"

"Exactly," I interrupted. "Or when you have a bad feeling before turning down a dark alley."

"Right. What people don't seem to understand is that everyday intuition is the most basic form of supernatural communication. They assume that there needs to be a huge 'sign from above' before they will believe it's happening to them." Madisyn wasn't usually a fan of "air quotes," but in this case she couldn't help herself.

"It seems to me that we're all born with intuitive abilities. Look at children—they don't have the same preconceived ideas about what is real or imagined. They just look at *all* of the information they are getting as part of their lives."

"Like imaginary friends." Madisyn smiled. "Who's to say that those friends don't exist? In fact, many of my best friends have been imaginary."

We both laughed.

"But then society tries to convince us that certain feelings aren't real," I noted. "Over time we're conditioned to deaden our feelings with huge intellectual calluses that give us only a fraction of the intuitive ability we're born with. Perhaps it was helpful during the past few centuries to put our intuitive gifts on hold, allowing us to evolve faster in the fields of science and technology."

"The gift of tunnel vision."

"Precisely. But isn't it time to get out our psychic loofahs and scrub off our intellectual calluses so we can become whole again? We now have computers and biotechnologies, but at what cost?"

"They should let *us* rule the world," Madisyn said dryly.

"Yeah—we could revamp the educational system and require formal metaphysical training for everyone. Starting with *Intuitive Finger Painting* in preschool and continuing through *Conscious*

Business and the Art of Soulful Finance for MBA candidates."

"Isn't all finger painting intuitive?"

"Exactly. But very little finance is soulful."

Madisyn nodded thoughtfully, and an impish smirk crept onto her face. "And once all the schools were fixed, we could outlaw mullets and gas guzzlers and hippie sandals . . ."

"Hey, wait! I like my hippie sandals!"

"I know you do." She rolled her eyes.

It was nice to see Madisyn in a lighthearted mood after all the intensity that had plagued the previous several months. There was nothing like a miscarriage to dampen a playful spirit.

At that moment a bright blue dragonfly appeared from nowhere and hovered between us. It floated for several seconds and turned from one of us to the other, appearing to look directly into our eyes.

I reflected on how Autumn had often revealed herself as a dragonfly in the past. "Did you see that?" I asked Madisyn after it had flown away. "It looked just like . . ."

Madisyn nodded as a knowing smile shaped her lips. "Speaking of such things . . ."

"What?"

"You know."

"Are you . . . ?"

"I am."

"Pregnant?" I wanted to be sure I was following the discussion.

"Of course, pregnant! What else would I be talking about? I peed on the stick just before we left the house—pluses all around. Although I've been pretty sure since yesterday."

"Wow." I gave her a hug. "Are you okay?"

She nodded, her eyes beginning to water.

"I'm sure it will be much easier this time." I did my best to comfort her through my embrace.

"I don't know," she whispered. "I hope so."

CHAPTER TWELVE

"It's a good sign that you're having so much nausea," Madisyn's obstetrician and every armchair physician we knew would opine. "It means the baby is healthy."

Of course, that didn't make my wife *feel* any better, especially after going days without consuming more than a tablespoon-sized gulp of water. By then I was spending multiple hours each day driving to and from every store in Ashland so I could gather anything rumored to curb nausea or be mild enough for Madisyn's stomach. She would have good days and bad, although the bad ones were quickly starting to outnumber the good.

Fortunately, she was having a good day when the eighteen-week ultrasound had been scheduled. We had gone to several imaging appointments during the first pregnancy, and each would result in more blood tests and medical appointments. But this was the first ultrasound of the second pregnancy, and we were both very excited.

Madisyn disrobed and reclined on the white-sheeted examining table, as she had before. The small linoleum room remained exactly as it had been previously, from the gallery of black-and-white fetus images lining the walls, to the imposing metallic-tubed cart barely containing all the computers, television monitors, and wires that would produce the images we had come for.

"Howdy!" the most chipper lab technician I'd ever seen squeaked as she bounced through the door while flipping through Madisyn's chart. "I see you came in for baby's first pictures!"

Her demeanor was much more suited to a preschool talent show than a doctor's office; however, on this day I appreciated her unrelenting optimism. During the multiple appointments connected with the first pregnancy, her personality had definitely worn thin, but since we were starting anew, it was good to be reminded of the joy we were hoping for.

"Should I put my feet in the stirrups?" My wife sighed in resignation, eyeing the invasive wand that she had become quite familiar with during previous visits.

"Let's try the old-fashioned way first." The technician giggled as she lifted Madisyn's gown and squeezed a tube of clear gel onto her lower belly. "Oops—that might be a bit chilly!"

She then retrieved a small brick-shaped paddle from its holster and began smearing the gel with the white plastic cube. The black-and-white television screen blinked to life. At first the monitor revealed the familiar scene of jumbled pixels we were used to from previous visits. I imagined a postmodern video artist hiding in the next room while muttering in a mock-French accent, "I call it *Snow Falling on Ocean #32.*"

Unexpectedly, the sea blizzard coalesced into an image resembling something much more recognizable.

It. Was. A. Baby.

"Do you see that?" I gasped while squeezing my wife's hand.

"Uh-huh."

The impersonal computer monitor had transformed into a miraculous window into the wonderland within my wife's belly, and there was no mistaking what was living inside—a squirming fetus with tiny arms, minuscule fingers, and a massive head that looked at least three times too big for the little body. Before, we had been lucky to see a darkened circle with a glowing halo, but this time it was a *baby.* A real baby. I was so enthralled that I forgot to breathe for several seconds.

Madisyn and I smiled at each other, and I could see tears of joy pooling at the corners of her eyes. Those tears said more than a four hundred–page novel could ever begin to capture. The joy. The relief. The hope. The surrender.

As the technician shifted the plastic cube, a bright light began pulsing in the center of the screen.

"What's that blinking?" Madisyn asked with a concerned tone.

"That's your baby's heart!" The technician giggled again as she began tapping on the attached keyboard. "One hundred fifty-three beats per minute."

"That seems like a lot—are you sure that's okay?"

"Perfectly normal. Your baby seems perfectly healthy in every way."

She then pressed a button and froze the image on the computer monitor and began drawing lines along different areas of the baby. Every time she would complete a line, she would mumble a measurement to herself and quickly enter it on the keyboard before unfreezing the image. As she continued, the images looked less like a baby and more like a study in abstract expressionism. The faux-French video artist was smiling again.

Rotate. Freeze. Draw. Measure. Type. Repeat.

It was impressive how quickly she was able to collect the array of measurements, although her gentle approach became decidedly more forceful as she began to dig the plastic cube deep into Madisyn's abdomen to get the final angles. In less than two minutes flat, she had collected enough measurements for an Italian tailor specializing in the finest of womb wear.

"Hmm." The technician's permanent smile faltered slightly as she pursed her lips.

"What's wrong?" asked Madisyn.

"Well, I should probably let your doctor tell you about this, but . . ." She paused as if to weigh the professional ramifications of spilling the beans.

". . . I'm just seeing a few unexplained masses that concern me."

"Oh, that's probably my fibroid," explained Madisyn. "I've had it for years."

"I'm sure that's it. It looks like it has a friend now—we should probably keep an eye on them from here on out."

"Can they cause problems?" I asked.

"The good news is, they're on the outside of the uterine wall. So as long as they don't move around and block the baby's exit, they shouldn't cause a problem . . ." Then, without warning, the technician gasped, and I felt my heart stop.

"Oh my!" she squeaked. "Isn't that the cutest thing ever!?"

She flipped a switch, and the translucent black-and-white picture instantly transformed into a golden claylike image that looked surprisingly more . . . *baby*like. All the miniature details came in crisp focus, and it was much easier to discern what she was talking about.

Our little baby was sucking its thumb.

"Awwww," the three of us chorused. It was almost painful how cute it was—it easily put the "Hang in there" kitty poster on the wall of the reception area to shame.

"That's a keeper!" the technician said as the thermal printer spat out a printout of the adorable pose. She continued to dig around Madisyn's abdomen with the plastic cube until she found more glamour shots of the baby that she could print out. In less than a minute the ultrasound machine had produced a narrow scroll of baby pictures that reached the floor.

Then the technician began to titter, and her smile widened. It was easy to see she was enjoying herself immensely—she obviously loved her job. When she could no longer contain herself, she finally asked, "Do you want to *know?*"

"Know what?" Madisyn asked, clearly concerned there was something wrong.

"The gender. Do you want to know if you're having a boy or a girl?"

"Sure," we both replied at the same time, shrugging. After all, we knew in our hearts that we were preparing to welcome Autumn into this world, and she had always made it known that she was a girl.

"It's a *boy!*" the technician shrieked.

"A what?" I must have misunderstood her.

"A boy."

"Are you sure?"

She laughed as she tapped the keyboard, enlarging the current image on the screen. She then used her mouse to draw a crude stick arrow pointing to what looked like a miniature church steeple between our baby's tiny legs. To make it even more obvious, she typed three capital letters next to the accusatory pointer: BOY.

"Congratulations!" The technician was now the only one keeping the energy up in the room. "Isn't that exciting?"

"Uh-huh," Madisyn muttered, looking nearly as shell-shocked as I felt.

I stared at the image on the screen for what seemed like hours as the rest of the room faded out of focus. I'm sure I would have passed out if I wasn't already sitting, but I just stared at the computer monitor until the technician shut off the ultrasound machine and flicked on the room lights. She smiled as she handed me the paper-clipped roll of photos she had printed and gently ushered us into the waiting room.

In the car, Madisyn and I didn't say a word during the ride home.

We both couldn't believe it was true.

At first it was easy to avoid the dreaded *B* word without too much effort. Dealing with Madisyn's nausea was a constant struggle, and finding food she could keep down had become nearly impossible. But when I had time to myself, I began to get seriously depressed. I wondered if I had done anything wrong to permanently scare Autumn away, or if my entire experience with her had been made up. Did I imagine the whole thing?

After nearly a week of silent self-torture, I couldn't hold it in any longer.

"I can't believe Autumn's not coming," I whispered to Madisyn, after removing yet another plate of uneaten food from the bedside table.

"Humph."

"I was so sure she was going to be our daughter. She told me so in that dream . . ."

Silence.

"Are you mad at me?"

More silence.

"So you *are* mad at me!"

"I'm not mad at you." She rolled her eyes. "Everything isn't about you. It's just that I've always wanted a little girl. I was *supposed* to have a girl. Ever since I was younger, I imagined what it would be like. How I would dress her. How I would decorate her room. What I would teach her. What we would do together. We were supposed to dress up for tea. I was supposed to have a girl."

Madisyn started to cry.

I felt terrible. Was I responsible for misleading her? By telling her about my dreams about Autumn? By being so sure of myself?

"Maybe the technician was wrong," I suggested hopefully. "Maybe it's really a girl."

"Wrong? How could she be wrong? It wasn't a blood test or a dream or something—she just looked! I saw it, you saw it, we all saw it!"

"I'm just saying . . . maybe the umbilical cord was in the way or something."

"Whatever. I just don't know what I'm going to do with a boy. It's not like *you* know what to do with a boy either."

"What do you mean by that?"

Silence.

"What do you mean by that?" I repeated.

"It's just . . . you *hate* boys." She started to cry again.

"Don't be ridiculous. I don't hate boys."

"Yes, you do. You haven't had a male friend since I've known you."

"I just relate better to women, that's all."

"Exactly. And how are you going to relate to your *son?*" She emphasized the last word like it was an accusation.

"I'm . . . just . . . it . . ."

"That's what I thought. All I know is, you better get over your childhood crap soon. You only have five months left."

CHAPTER THIRTEEN

Madisyn was right.

I did have a lot of childhood crap to get over. And it scared me to death that I only had five months before I finally needed to let it go. Once again my anxiety dreams returned with a vengeance, and every night I began to dread what memories would be dredged up from my past.

Old man Thatcher owned the largest pumpkin patch in Scott Valley. Every year before Halloween, he and his ranch hands would generously deliver a truckful of ripe pumpkins to the school for the children to bring home.

Coming from the city, I was excited about this unique community outreach and looked forward to it for weeks.

The pumpkin selection was a predictably chaotic affair, as each grade was given three minutes to browse the makeshift pumpkin patch that had taken over the school parking lot. The girls' gym teacher armed herself with the same piercing whistle and blue plastic stopwatch that she used when officiating interschool track meets.

"Each student is allotted one pumpkin only, so choose carefully," she yelled in her husky voice. "You have exactly three minutes to select your pumpkin and bring it back to the steps. One. Pumpkin. Only."

The students in my class lined up at the opening of the roped-off parking lot and eagerly awaited the whistle.

"On your mark. Get set. Go!"

As soon as the whistle blew, I was nearly trampled by the crowd of eager pumpkin hunters behind me. I attempted to compete with the first string of gatherers, but every time I got near a pumpkin I liked, it was quickly snatched up by more experienced hands. After searching through dozens of misshapen pumpkins that looked more like deformed gourds than potential jack-o'-lanterns, I finally found the one I was looking for. It had a classic shape, was an unusually vibrant shade of reddish orange, and had the smoothest skin I had ever seen on a fruit or vegetable.

It was perfect.

I carefully carried it to my locker and patiently waited for the final school bell to ring so I could bring it home. My family had a tradition of carving pumpkins and roasting their seeds each Halloween, and I had convinced them to wait until this very evening so I would be able to carve one from Thatcher's farm.

Nearly everyone in school had selected a pumpkin that day, and most ended up taking up an entire seat on the bus ride home. Friends who usually paired off were spread out among as many seats, and although there were plenty to be had, I ended up near the back of the bus for the first time since the puka-shell incident.

The last student to get on the bus was Jim. He was carrying two large pumpkins, one under each arm, as he made his way toward me.

"We're going to have some fun!" he exclaimed as he sat down in the empty seat

behind me. I didn't know what he was up to, but I had a feeling I wouldn't like it.

Once the bus was out of town and moving at full speed on the open highway, Jim slid his window open and proclaimed, "It's time!"

I turned around as he shoved his first pumpkin out the open window, and I watched in astonishment as it plummeted onto the pavement behind us. It bounced three feet into the air before struggling to keep up with us. There was something compelling about the way the orange gourd rolled behind us at thirty-five miles per hour, chasing the bus with intense determination, its stem spinning around in a green blur. Without warning, the pumpkin split in half and continued to trail us, like two wheels held by an invisible axle. The pumpkin fragments succeeded for about a hundred yards before exploding into a thousand pieces all over the highway.

It was amazing.

Before the remains of the first pumpkin were out of sight, Jim tossed the second onto the road, after covertly checking that the bus driver wasn't watching. It followed the same fate as the first, and within seconds, several kids had passed their pumpkins to the back of the bus so Jim could annihilate them in the same way he had his own.

Bounce. Roll. Split. Explode.

The Execution of the Exploding Pumpkins lasted for nearly the entire ride home, and Jim's ebullient mood didn't sour until he ran out of victims. Once his cache was empty, he eagerly slid next to me and held out his hands.

"Uh . . . um," I stammered. "I want to keep mine."

"Don't be stupid!" he responded. "Give it here!"

Jim grabbed the prickly green stem and yanked on it hard, until it came off in his calloused hand. He then tried to wrestle the pumpkin away from me, but I was able to retain my grip by using my entire upper body as a vise.

Crunch.

His fist connected with my nose in an explosion of pain and astonishment that temporarily stunned me. My ears rang like a hissing ocean, and my eyes saw nothing but a sea of inky blackness twinkling with reddish-yellow glitter.

When my vision returned, I saw several streams of blood slowly trickling down the smooth orange skin of my pumpkin. And the divot left by the liberated stem was quickly filling up with a pool of bright red liquid dripping from my nose.

"What's wrong with you?!" Jim yelled as he grabbed the bloody pumpkin away from me and tossed it out the window.

Perhaps Madisyn had a point—maybe I did hate boys. I certainly hated all the ugly things that boys did in the name of manliness. I hated the senseless macho behavior that led to fistfights and bloody noses. I hated the misogynistic excuses that justified treating women as second-class citizens. I hated the testosterone-fueled violent rampages that destroyed innocent lives. But most of all, I hated myself for being genetically sympathetic to the masculine plight.

I hated myself for being a boy.

CHAPTER FOURTEEN

The next several weeks were filled with disquiet and anxiety over the gender of our baby. We both knew that we were being selfish, but we also felt it was important to work through our feelings completely before he was born instead of harboring lingering uncertainty after he arrived.

"At least he's healthy," I offered. "You know how many kids are born with birth defects or incurable diseases?"

Madisyn nodded. "And we're lucky that we were able to conceive in the first place."

"True." I sighed. "I just feel so guilty that I'm having these feelings in light of everything that other people go through. Am I no different from the barbaric cultures that kill their babies when they turn out to be girls?"

"You want to *kill* him?!"

"Of course not!" I was horrified that she could even think I would suggest such a thing. "I'm just wondering if we should have tried at different times of your cycle or given you foods that would have helped prepare your uterus for a girl."

"What *are* you reading?" She laughed.

"I should probably throw that book away." I smiled. "I guess the universe always gives us exactly what we need."

"Maybe." She shrugged. "All I know is that *you* are going to teach him about sex."

"I figured."

"And how to pee standing up."

On an unusually crisp fall morning in early November, Madisyn woke up with a serene look on her face. For weeks she hadn't had any relief from her constant nausea, and the anxiety about having a boy was starting to take its toll on both of us. But on that day she was in an uncharacteristically good mood and eager to share something important.

"He told me his name," she whispered quietly.

"*Who* told you his name?" Her words took me by surprise, since our recent morning conversations had traditionally been limited to what foods she might be able to keep down that day.

"Who do you think?" She gestured with her eyes to her growing belly.

"Oh, really? What did he say?"

"He said that everything was going to be all right. That he picked us to be his parents because he knew we would be perfect for him. That we would do a good job. And that he wanted his name to be Oliver."

"Oliver?"

"Yes."

There was something about the name that bothered me. I struggled with what I was feeling, but I couldn't pinpoint it. Even though I didn't understand my antipathy, I finally shrugged and said, "That's kind of old-fashioned, isn't it?"

My words visibly annoyed Madisyn, and her good mood quickly faded. I could tell she was disappointed that I wasn't as excited about the name as she was. "Well, I like it."

Then it occurred to me what I was bothered by. It wasn't about the name at all—it was about Autumn. I had spent the past few years waiting for my daughter to appear, and in her place was an impostor—a charlatan who called himself Oliver and who had the audacity to take my daughter's place. It wasn't about the name at all. It was about the name making it more real that *she* wasn't coming.

"I just had a thought," I said, trying to muster some enthusiasm. "Maybe it really is Autumn, but she decided to choose a male body instead."

"I already thought about that," replied Madisyn. "But that doesn't feel right to me—the energy of Oliver is much different. I feel like I recognize his soul, but he's definitely not the same baby I was carrying before."

Then a familiar voice echoed in my head. For the first time since Madisyn had become pregnant again, Autumn spoke to me.

She's right. That's not me.

Although Madisyn's nausea continued to worsen, her emotional health gradually recovered once she had talked with Oliver. I envied how at peace she was with his gender, while my own internal struggle was still afoot. What made it worse was that I felt I couldn't talk to anyone about it. In the past I had been able to confide in Madisyn, but she needed all the strength she had; and besides, *she* was the one carrying him. It was understood that he needed to be nurtured in every way through his fetal development, and getting mired in doubts about his gender couldn't be good for him during this fragile process.

I was embarrassed by the feelings I was having and couldn't imagine anyone sympathizing with a father-to-be who was bringing a healthy baby boy into a stable and loving home. Why couldn't I just be happy for the miracle that was unfolding in our lives?

What was wrong with me?

When I couldn't handle going through it by myself any longer, I called Martika and told her the entire story. She already knew most of it, but I could tell she was surprised that I was still having such a hard time dealing with the baby's gender.

She understood that I was disappointed that Autumn wasn't coming; however, she also told me that she couldn't imagine why I would want to dissociate myself from half the human race. At first I thought she was being overly dramatic, but after a while I realized she was probably right. Maybe I did think the world would be a better place if only females inhabited it.

Over the next few weeks, I buried myself in research conducted by various radical philosophers and artists who were asking the same question. Evidently there was a very real debate going on as to whether males were currently being phased out of the human race because they were no longer needed from an evolutionary standpoint.

Then one day, Martika phoned me unexpectedly and suggested that I come to her house immediately. She had someone staying with her I needed to meet.

When I arrived, she excitedly told me more about her guest.

"I'm hosting a retreat this weekend with the most amazing man. His name is Andrew Harvey, and he's . . . oh, how would I describe him? I guess you would call him a mystic-scholar. He was born in India, educated at Oxford, studied with amazing Indian and Turkish gurus, and is now one of the most revered translators of Rumi in the world."

"Wow, he sounds amazing. Is that what your retreat is about . . . Rumi?" I hadn't read much by the Persian poet but was definitely a fan of what I'd seen.

"Not this time. He's also a leading expert on the subject of the Divine Feminine. That's what he's talking about this weekend."

"That's ironic," I snorted.

"What do you mean?"

"A *man* being an expert on femininity. Isn't it a bit presumptuous that someone who isn't female could be an *expert* on something that's inherently not masculine?"

"I never really thought of it that way." She shrugged. "He's gay, if that helps."

"Ah, maybe that's the answer," I joked. "Maybe I'd be more comfortable having a son if he were gay. It would be so much easier if he kissed boys, don't you think?"

"Maybe for you"—she smiled—"but society in general still doesn't treat everyone as equally as we would like."

"Well, that's just silly." I waved off her assertion with my hand. "Why would anyone care what someone else does in their personal life?"

"Look who's talking." She laughed. "You're the one trying to impose a sexual preference on your unborn child."

"Touché."

At that moment, a dapper gentleman dressed in a light blue button-down shirt and dark blazer strolled into the kitchen where we had been talking. His salt-and-pepper hair was unkempt like a mad professor, and his flowing gestures were simultaneously childlike and graceful.

"Good afternoon, my dear Martika," he said with a refined English accent. "The room you have so graciously prepared for me is ab-so-lute-ly exquisite. Those little soaps are magical, aren't they?"

"Andrew, I'd like to introduce you to my good friend Scott."

"Ah yes—the expectant father, I presume." He extended his hand and shook mine formally. "Martika has been telling me about you and your wife's circuitous journey to parenthood. Will she be joining us?"

"No, my wife's been having a very difficult pregnancy. With the previous miscarriage and now her unrelenting nausea, she's had a pretty bad year."

"Oh, that's dreadful! Absolutely atrocious! I'm so sorry to hear that. I will pray for her tonight before I retire."

"Thank you."

"Andrew," Martika spoke up, "Scott has been having some fascinating thoughts on the subject of gender that you might be interested in."

"Um . . . yeah," I stammered. "Thanks, Martika."

I felt uncomfortable sharing my innermost anxieties with someone I'd just met, and was somewhat annoyed that Martika had offered on my behalf without even asking me.

Andrew patiently waited, his childlike eyes sparkling with anticipation. There was something about him that drew me in, although his air of sophistication was also quite intimidating. I toyed with the idea of steering the conversation toward something less relevant, but decided to jump right in.

"I guess I feel most comfortable with women," I said after a deep breath. "Their gentle demeanor seems to be more in alignment with my soul than many of the men I've met."

Andrew nodded sympathetically.

"And over the years," I continued, "I've found myself surrounded almost exclusively by females.

It's not something I consciously seek to perpetuate; it just seems to happen naturally. Of course, my wife isn't a big fan of the fact that most of my friends are women, but she also seems to appreciate that I can relate to her on that level."

"You're in touch with your feminine side," Andrew suggested.

"Perhaps . . . but when we found out that we were having a boy, it ultimately made me question how relevant gender is in this day and age. Splitting the duties between men and women made a lot of sense when our society was less developed. But in today's world, with many needs being met by grocery stores, technology, and medical advances, it seems like dividing the human race along gender lines is no longer relevant.

"From a purely practical standpoint, females are obviously the ones who bear children, and the process of artificial insemination, gathered from a few male 'servants' in a sperm farm, should be able to perpetuate the human race indefinitely. Women are clearly in the driver's seat now, and it all seems to invite the ultimate question: *Are men still necessary?*"

"You just said a mouthful, my dear boy." Andrew chuckled as he sipped the vanilla rooibos tea that Martika had prepared before leaving us alone in the kitchen. "But it's not the gender differences of our flesh clothing where the war is being waged. It is *within* each of us that the exquisite tension of both the Divine Feminine and Divine Masculine struggle to find balance with one another.

"Inside all of us are the feminine powers of intuition, patience, and nurturing, in addition to the masculine energies of rule, reason, and protection. Within this division, the ultimate objective is the Sacred Marriage that weds the Divine Feminine to the Divine Masculine and will eventually bear the exquisite fruit of the Divine Androgyne. That is what will awaken us to our full potential and allow us to embody *divine love in action.*

"As the great Sufi mystic and poet Jalal-ud-Din Rumi committed to parchment:

When man and woman become one, You are that Unity.
You have created this 'I' and 'Us'
To play the game of adoration with Yourself;
All the 'I's' and 'You's' will become one single soul
And in the end melt into the Beloved."

"That's a beautiful poem," I commented. "I definitely need to read more Rumi. But I believe you just proved my point. The human race is heading toward a single gender—and whether feminine or androgynous, it is clearly not masculine. And you can't deny the scientific fact that the world now has more females than males. If that isn't a telling nod to Darwin, I don't know what is."

"The ultimate goal of balance is not to calcify into a perpetual state of being. It is the very *tension* of balance itself that is embodied by the beauty of gender." Raising his voice, Andrew began to gesture passionately and nearly knocked his teacup off the table. "Thank God there are currently more women than men at this crucial time of our evolution! It's imperative that the pendulum swing in the opposite direction in order to finally *shatter* the male-dominated society that has corrupted our souls and threatened to obliterate our very species!

"Yes, now is the time for the fullest restoration of the powers, passions, and glories of the Divine Feminine—to reclaim what has been violently ripped from her breast by our masculine brethren. But that does not mean that she will claim victory in the form of a singular gender. No, she is much too perceptive to fall into that quagmire. She can see clearly that our path leads to the altar of the Sacred Marriage."

"But in this coming age of the Divine Feminine, why would I want my child to be born male?" I asked. "Isn't it ingrained in every parent to want the best for their child and to provide them every advantage possible? By being born into a time when women are in the process of reclaiming their power previously stolen by men, doesn't it put the new generation of males at an obvious disadvantage?"

"Now I understand where this is born from," Andrew replied. "It is because of your very nature that you are blessed with the ability to *feel* this reclamation in the depths of your tender soul. But what you don't realize is that the war has already been won, dear boy. The Divine Feminine has claimed victory, and we are already in the midst of transitioning to feminine rule. The only problem is, the masculine elite haven't realized it yet. All they know is that the old paradigm is crumbling beneath their feet, and they are grasping at the final shards of what had been built on the backs of the less fortunate. Their world will continue to crumble until the old paradigm is finally laid to waste in an inconsolable pile of rubble. Then and only then will the Divine Feminine rebuild the world in her image, and the pendulum will have officially swung in the opposite direction.

"And that is where your son comes in. The world no longer needs any more feminine warriors to fight a battle that has already been won. Now it is necessary for a new generation of souls that embody purity and the original intention of the Divine Masculine to help bring the world back into balance. And it is to your son's credit that he picked you and your wife as parents, because of your acute awareness of the importance of his charge. You have been given the colossal responsibility of offering guidance and compassion on this difficult and wholly essential mission of love."

I sipped my tea in silence, letting Andrew's powerful words sink in. I wasn't sure if I understood everything he had said, but I couldn't deny that his words took the edge off my anxiety about the gender of our child. For the first time I felt an authentic optimism about having a boy.

I was finally excited to meet Oliver.

Later that night I had a vivid dream.

I was riding a spotted Appaloosa along the edge of a plateau at twilight. The muscular horse was marked with red clay, and around his eye was a painted crimson circle.

This wasn't the first time I had dreamed that I was living in the time of my Native American ancestors, but it was the first time I'd ever felt the agonizing heaviness of war in my heart. However, it wasn't a war of anger and passion that I was feeling, but of loss and sadness. It didn't concern me that my life might end on that day, but I was overwhelmingly disheartened by the fact that many of my loved ones would also suffer the same fate.

As I approached a picturesque bluff overlooking the valley, I saw the one I had come to meet—a young warrior, dressed similarly to myself. He wore a sleeveless buckskin vest adorned with hand-painted images of eagles and stars, a single eagle feather affixed to his long ebony braids, and two broad strokes of red paint on his face. But his exquisite eyes were most striking of all. They sparkled in the rising moonlight with the depth of a thousand oceans, simultaneously straddling ancient times and the distant future. The handsome warrior was undeniably a member of my soul family from generations past, and would continue to be for generations to come.

Before he said a word, I knew in my heart when I would see him again. The connection was too deep, too immediate, too powerful, to deny. When I looked into his eyes, I could tell I was seeing both my past and my future, like a Celtic snake feeding on its own tail.

"Tonight you will learn my name," he uttered in a somber voice. His dialect was unfamiliar, although every word was clearly understood.

"I know your name." I smiled. "You're Oliver."

"That is my given name," he replied gravely. "Tonight you will learn my second name—my spirit name."

Before I could reply, his painted pony sprinted ahead, and mine skillfully cantered in their wake. We rode along the narrow pathway overlooking the carnage that had already begun in the valley below. Enemies had set fire to our village, and although our families were temporarily hidden in the adjacent brush, little time remained before we would need to join our brethren and fulfill our duty.

We arrived at the bank of a shallow pond that I recognized as a favorite place from childhood. Memories flooded in of splashing the water during warm summer days and drinking from the crystal clear spring that bubbled up from the forest floor. The water remained black as pitch until the moonbeams filtered through the trees and shed silvery light onto the pond's surface. The full moon continued to ascend until it was clearly visible above our heads, and a rippled facsimile floated just a few feet from our horses' hooves.

"My second name," he said as he gestured to the shimmering reflection in front of us.

I paused to let the moment etch itself deeply into my soul before saying the word out loud: "Moon."

He nodded. "You must carry my spirit name deep within your heart and return it to me when I see you again."

I humbly bowed my head, and he turned his horse to begin riding across the plateau and into the valley. His distinctive battle cry entwined with bloodcurdling screams rising from below as he galloped toward the burning village. I resolutely followed, without a thought for my safety.

It was my honor.

Winter moon rises,
while lighting the sky.

Turning the tides.

CHAPTER FIFTEEN

Time accelerated at light speed during the next month, which was filled with weekly doctor's visits and a constant barrage of last-minute preparations for our pending arrival. Madisyn and I were both obsessed with making everything as perfect as possible, and every day came with a new list of supplies to obtain and improvements to make on the nursery.

The due date was scheduled for two days before the end of winter, which had always made me slightly uncomfortable. My favorite season was springtime, and it seemed so much more poetic for our first child to be born when nature began its own cycle of rebirth. If we could convince Oliver to hold off a few more days, he could celebrate his birthday at the same time that Mother Earth did.

However, when the equinox passed and the cherry blossoms were fully in bloom, we had a much larger concern.

"You're no more dilated than last time," Dr. Carducci noted after our fifth weekly checkup. "We can go a few more days, but I'm concerned that your body won't naturally be able to initiate labor. It seems likely that your fibroid has shifted and is preventing your baby's head from pressing against the cervix to begin the process."

"What can be done?" I asked, although we had already discussed all the possibilities at length during the previous visit.

"At this point there are two options," she repeated patiently. "We can induce labor with medication and hope the body takes over—or we can prepare for a C-section."

"Is he ready to come out?" I asked pointedly, not trying to hide my concern. "Are you sure he's fully baked?"

"Yes." She smiled. "I'm absolutely confident he's ready."

"What happens if my body doesn't take over after you administer the Pitocin?" Madisyn asked with the inquisitiveness of a medical student.

"That's what I'm concerned about. If your fibroid is blocking the cervix, like I believe, then we'll end up having to surgically remove him anyway."

"You mean I'll go into labor *and* have a C-section?"

"Unfortunately, that seems likely."

"When's the earliest we could schedule the surgery?"

"I called the hospital just before you arrived and reserved the delivery room for tomorrow morning. You don't have to take it, but you'll probably need to make a decision in the next few days."

I looked at my wife sitting on the examining table, and was surprised to sense a wave of serenity wash over her. Ever since we had first discussed having a baby, she had been steadfast in her insistence that the birth be as natural as possible, and a Cesarean section was the absolute last thing on the agenda. Since I had been born via C-section, I was less against the idea; however, I wasn't the one whose body was being cut into. I had expected a huge fight if this day ever came to pass, but to my wife's credit, she had fully surrendered to whatever was going to happen.

"Okay, let's do it tomorrow," Madisyn said calmly. "It's time to get him out of me."

March 31, 4:28 A.M.

Neither of us was able to sleep that night, so it wasn't difficult to get out of bed before the alarm began its annoying assault. Everything had already been impeccably organized into Ziplocs and duffel bags, so it only took a few minutes to pack everything into the car.

As I stood in the driveway under the starlit sky, I looked back at the house Madisyn and I shared and realized that our life was about to change forever. We were leaving our life as a couple behind, and when we next returned to our home, we would officially be a family of three.

When I saw the silhouette of my pregnant wife standing in the doorway, a profound sense of loss welled up inside of me that nearly drove out the flock of butterflies that had taken residence in my stomach. I was excited to meet my new son, but I also felt a sense of sadness about losing the exclusive relationship that my soul mate and I had built over the years.

Neither of us uttered a word as we got into the car and silently drove through the empty streets of Ashland. Language couldn't capture the intense emotions we were both feeling.

5:03 A.M.

Martika met us at the emergency-room entrance, and the admitting nurse was already expecting us. After signing a small forest of paper, we were led through a labyrinth of fluorescent-lit hallways to the maternity wing.

We crowded into a tiny room, and after Madisyn changed into her backless gown, a blur of hospital personnel shuffled through the room with the precision of an assembly line. Each person had a distinct job to do; one inserted a large needle into the back of her hand, another attached an intravenous tube to a bag, and another affixed a plastic-covered ID bracelet that held two additional tiny bracelets for Oliver to her wrist. By the time the fifth assistant squeezed into the available space next to my wife's bedside, I was no longer able to track all the tasks being executed by the floral-print army.

5:51 A.M.

After Madisyn had been sufficiently readied, a nurse handed Martika and me each a bundle of folded blue hospital scrubs. She directed us to put them on promptly and be ready to go in the next half hour.

"Also, be sure to have the music ready that you want to play during the birth," the nurse casually mentioned as she was leaving. "We'll be asking for it soon."

Panic overtook me as I tried to remember if I had brought the disc with me. I had been given one simple task to be responsible for—and I'd already screwed it up.

"I'm going to get the bags," I said, feigning confidence. "The music's in the car."

I hurriedly followed the illuminated exit signs through the linoleum maze until I found the double glass doors to the parking lot. I sprinted to the car and shuffled through the luggage before finding the disc in the bag that Madisyn had packed herself.

R. Carlos Nakai.

We had both wholeheartedly agreed that an instrumental album by the Native American master flutist would be the first music Oliver would ever hear. There was something ineffably divine about the musician's soulful breath that felt wholly primal and worthy of such a momentous occasion. Even the song names seemed appropriate to welcome a new soul into the world, beginning with "Song for the Morning Star" and ending with "Homage to the Ancient Ones."

I clutched the jewel case with my left hand and gathered as many bags as I could carry with my right before run-waddling back to the room.

6:07 A.M.

After finding my way back to the maternity wing, I entered the room and saw Martika sitting on the corner of the bed dressed in blue scrubs.

"You better get dressed," Martika urged. "The nurse said they'll be back any minute to take her to the delivery room."

The simple task of putting on the scrubs seemed daunting once I closed the door of the undersized bathroom. I stood frozen for several minutes while looking at the frightened boy staring back at me in the small mirror. "I don't know what to do," he insisted. "What am I supposed to do?"

You better get dressed, Martika's words echoed in my brain. I pulled the cotton elastic-waisted pants over my jeans, and removing the Mother Mary T-shirt I'd worn for good luck, put on the matching V-neck.

I attempted to regain my composure before entering the room, and found Madisyn resting peacefully with her eyes shut.

"You okay?" Martika whispered while reassuringly touching my arm.

I nodded silently, fighting the wave of emotion swelling inside of me. I was overwhelmed by the idea that every moment on that important day would set the tone for how I would be as a father for the rest of my life. But the only thing I knew for sure was that I knew absolutely nothing. I had no idea what I was supposed to do and was utterly terrified by the thought of holding our baby for the first time.

Thankfully, Martika was there and would show me what to do.

6:23 A.M.

"Okay, Mama," Dr. Carducci whispered sweetly while stroking my wife's belly. "It's time to get this baby out of you."

It was nice to see a familiar face among the herd of medical personnel who had swarmed Madisyn's bed. With razor-sharp precision, dozens of tubes and wires were disassembled and reattached to ready the wheeled hospital bed for takeoff.

Before I could say a word, my wife was being rolled down the hallway deep into the belly of the hospital, while Martika and I hurried behind. My mind dizzied as we passed through Pediatrics, Oncology, Radiology, and Pathology and finally ended up in an open corridor before a pair of ominous steel doors. The sign attached to the wall above the industrial molding stated clearly: DELIVERY ROOM 2: SISKIYOU ROOM.

"You two need to stay here while the patient is being prepared," the nurse who'd been minding the stern of the bed "vessel" explained. "You're welcome to make yourself comfortable in the bull pen while you wait."

I felt helpless watching my wife being wheeled through the double doors into the brightly lit room. I looked at Martika and shrugged before following her into the "bull pen." The glass-walled office was outfitted with three ergonomically designed workstations complete with desktop computers and gunmetal filing cabinets. We waited silently in the dimly lit room, which felt more like a generic corporate work space than anything having to do with a hospital.

6:48 A.M.

After several minutes of watching me silently pace the available floor space between cubicles, Martika called my attention to "Nurse Stern," who was leaving the delivery room. She entered the bull pen holding a clipboard, apparently checking off last-minute preparations.

Without looking up, she uttered in a detached monotone, "I'm here for the music you want to play during the delivery."

I handed her the disc, and she made a note on her clipboard before continuing her emotionless recital. "And to clarify, there is only *one guest* allowed in the delivery room. I'm assuming the father will be joining us today?"

"Excuse me?" I heard myself say as I felt the color drain from my face and onto the tiled floor. "Dr. Carducci told us that we could have two guests in the delivery room."

"I was just in the delivery room with Dr. Carducci, and she understands that the rule is that only one guest is allowed to be present during a Cesarean section. There's scarcely enough room for a single guest with all the personnel and equipment needed today."

"I thought it was at the doctor's discretion how many guests were allowed in."

"No," she said firmly, without hiding her annoyance. "The *anesthesiologist* has the final decision regarding all discretionary policies. And he was very clear today—there is only room for one guest. If there is a problem . . ."

"There's not a problem," Martika calmly interrupted. "We completely understand. I'm sure you can appreciate that tensions are high at the moment."

"So, can I assume that the *father* will be joining us in the delivery room today?" the nurse snidely repeated.

By this point I was so angry that I was afraid to speak in case I said something that would get me thrown out of the hospital altogether. Thankfully, Martika replied on my behalf.

"Yes, thank you."

The nurse turned on her heel and stomped out of the bull pen and disappeared into the delivery room.

"Can you believe that?!" I exclaimed once she was out of earshot. "If I had known you weren't allowed in, I wouldn't have asked you to come. I'm so sorry you had to get up so early."

"Even if I'd known for sure that I wouldn't be allowed in, I would've come anyway." She smiled. "I wouldn't have missed it for the world."

My paralyzing anxiety about holding the newborn baby returned with a vengeance. I still didn't know what to do, and the only way I had convinced myself it would be tolerable was if Martika was there to help. With Madisyn sedated for surgery, I was terrified that I would be expected to know what to do and nobody would help me. What if I hurt him? What if I dropped him? What would happen if I told them that I *wouldn't* hold him—that I didn't know how? Would they report me to Child Protective Services? Would they take our baby away from us if I didn't know what to do? How could I be a father if I didn't even know how to *hold* him?

"How are you feeling?" Martika asked softly.

The jumble of emotions was so overwhelming that it was nearly impossible to pick apart.

Intimidated. Excited. Nervous. Humbled. Disconnected. Apprehensive. Enthusiastic. Terrified. Scared. To. Death.

"I don't know," I finally answered. "It's just so big."

"It *is* big. You're about to become a daddy."

7:26 A.M.

Dr. Carducci burst through the double doors and jogged into the bull pen.

"Come on, you two," she said excitedly. "We're about to start. Scrub up to your elbows and put on your masks."

"But . . . but the nurse said Martika wasn't allowed in," I stammered. "She said the anesthesiologist wouldn't allow it."

"I talked with him and everything's fine. He just had a little scare yesterday when a family of five crowded a patient so he wasn't able to see what he was doing. Just give him room, and be mindful of where you're standing."

We followed Dr. Carducci into the delivery room after washing our hands in a hefty stainless-steel sink operated by convenient foot pedals. Nurse Stern was right—there was very little available space left surrounding the bed, with all of the equipment and people crowding my wife.

A large sheet of blue fabric was suspended above Madisyn, which served to shield her head from the rest of her body. There was also a clear plastic tube feeding oxygen to her nose and a cumbersome plastic *oximeter* that pinched her index finger while feeding vital information to the grumpy anesthesiologist standing behind us.

Before taking my place beside my wife, I stood on my tiptoes to look over the blue screen and glimpsed Dr. Carducci as she positioned a shining metal scalpel over Madisyn's lower belly. My wife's torso had been covered with a thin yellow plastic film that curiously dehumanized the exposed flesh.

"You shouldn't feel any pain," said Dr. Carducci, "but you might experience some pressure and a tugging sensation once we get started. If you feel any discomfort at all, let the anesthesiologist know immediately and he'll take care of you."

I held on to my wife's thumb and gently caressed her arm as the room went ominously silent. After a few seconds, a look of sheer terror came over Madisyn as her body began rocking back and forth. Her eyelids flung open wide as she gasped for air, and her face turned white.

"She's feeling pain!" I exclaimed.

"I see her," replied the anesthesiologist calmly and adjusted a few knobs on his blinking control center. Madisyn immediately relaxed and let her eyelids return to their shuttered state.

Instinctively, I stood up to see what had caused the discomfort and saw a baby's head poking through the incision in my wife's belly. At first it was surreal seeing a disembodied pink head floating above a sea of yellow plastic film, but when it moved and he opened his mouth, it became all too real.

7:41 A.M.

"I see him!" I whispered to Madisyn. "He's almost out."

"Is he okay?" she croaked, her voice barely perceptible through the anesthetic haze.

"He's perfect," I replied. I stood up again and peeked over the blue curtain. The tiny baby was covered in a milky viscous liquid, and the doctor was clearing his mouth with a rubber suction bulb. "Oh my God, he's completely out now!"

"Call it!" said the male nurse assisting Dr. Carducci.

"Seven forty-one." I recognized the voice of Nurse Stern and looked over to see her intently scribbling on her clipboard.

After his throat was clear, the newborn tried out his new lungs by letting out a faint cry that sounded more like a tentative greeting than a howl. His second "word" was much more insistent, and soon the operating room had filled with his resolute voice.

My elation was briefly tempered as I witnessed the tall male nurse unceremoniously cutting the umbilical cord after abruptly clamping it with yellow barrettes. *How rude,* I thought. *Dr. Carducci promised me that I was going to do that!* And then in a blur, the baby was whisked to the opposite end of the delivery room, where a clear acrylic tray filled with a mattress of white towels was awaiting him.

"Where's Daddy?" a soft-voiced nurse called out. "Baby wants to meet his daddy."

I left my wife's side to join two nurses intently focused on the newborn. They were both busy cleaning him up and checking to make sure everything was functioning properly. When I was able to see the infant up close, I was astonished to discover how mature he was. He looked less like a newborn and more like a miniature boy, with a full head of hair, a perfect button nose, and tiny fingernails that already looked like they needed a trim.

I tentatively reached into the acrylic tray, and when my fingers lightly caressed his soft hand, an enormous surge of energy nearly knocked me onto the floor. I felt as if I had been plugged into a high-voltage electrical socket that pulsed its tingling current throughout my entire body. He must have sensed that I was about to pull away, as he wrapped his tiny hand around my right index finger and held on to me with all his might. I gasped with joy, and marveled that his fingers were collectively unable to cover a single one of my own fingernails.

In that instant, a library full of memories flowed into my soul through our connected fingers. My heart filled with a recognition that was so deep that in that moment, I was unable to remember when I *hadn't* known him.

I could sense that there were others watching our interaction, and when I looked up to smile at the small audience that had gathered, I saw someone new who hadn't been in the delivery room before.

A young girl with flowing auburn hair was smiling at me from the opposite side of the acrylic tray. She had pulled herself up by standing on the nearby stainless-steel cart and was peeking over the lid of the tray between the two nurses. Her quasi-transparent form was a clue that she wasn't fully incarnate, although her energetic presence was so palpable that I almost reached out to touch her.

I came to see my brother, whispered Autumn. *To make sure he arrived safely.*

Her blue-green eyes revealed an ocean of history between her and her sibling, and I knew in my heart that she had been with him for much longer than the preceding nine months. With her thoughts she showed me images of their previous life in the spirit world together. I was humbled to witness the reunion of two souls that so dearly cared for one another.

Autumn smiled at me, before leaning over to delicately kiss the forehead of her newborn brother. His eyelids fluttered in recognition, but they remained shut under the glare of the brightly lit operating room. She then quietly whispered something in her brother's ear . . . before fading away.

"Prepare the mother," called the nurse, after expertly swaddling the newborn in a thin white blanket and matching knit cap. I needed to learn how to do that myself, but she moved too fast for me to follow all the folds and tucks.

I returned to my wife's side just as the nurse arrived with the precious bundle. The baby instantly relaxed into the crook of his mother's arm, and she beamed with a divine radiance that was so exquisitely gorgeous that she took my breath away. When we first met, I'd fallen in love with *Madisyn the Maiden,* after witnessing how her natural beauty and loving heart could fill any room she walked into. But even after years of sharing my life with her, nothing could prepare me for that moment of transcendent beauty when she first met Oliver.

In that instant I fell deeply in love with *Madisyn the Mother*—the mother of our child.

8:08 A.M.

"We need to let Dr. Carducci finish sewing you up," the nurse whispered to Madisyn after she was done nursing. "It looks like your good little eater had a healthy dose of colostrum, so we need to get you into recovery while he's in between snacks. Daddy and I will get him weighed and measured, and then we'll all join you as soon as you're finished—okay?"

Madisyn looked heartbroken when the nurse picked up the baby cocoon and began to walk out of the delivery room. I tenderly kissed my wife's forehead to say goodbye before Martika and I joined the nurse who was waiting for us in the hallway.

"You should stay with the mother," the nurse told Martika. "She's going to need a friendly face while she's readied for the recovery room."

My friend smiled at the three of us before leaving us alone in the hallway and returning to the delivery room. Once again my prebirth anxiety returned, and I almost called after Martika when I realized I would finally be expected to hold the baby. My fears were confirmed as we walked through the hospital hallway.

"One of the most important things to be done immediately after the baby leaves the womb is *skin-to-skin* contact," the nurse explained. "It helps keep the baby regulated to a naturally warm temperature, calms him down, and gently exposes him to normal bacteria, which will help protect him from harmful germs. Traditionally, we prefer skin-to-skin with the mother, but in the case of a C-section, when that isn't possible, studies have shown that the father is a suitable surrogate. And besides, it's a magnificent time to bond with your baby."

Oh great, I thought. *Now my insecurities are putting my own newborn's life at risk.*

"Okay," the nurse said as we entered a smaller version of the bull pen. "Let's get this little guy weighed and measured."

She expertly unwrapped the blanket as quickly as she had put it on and placed the newborn gently onto a curved stainless-steel tray perched atop a bright red digital readout.

"Seven pounds, eight ounces," she chirped. She quickly scribbled on her clipboard as he began to cry. "There, there," she said, picking him up and rubbing his back, "we're almost done, and then you can go to Daddy."

She then laid the baby on a towel-covered bench and began measuring him with a white cloth measuring tape.

"Twenty-one inches long," said the nurse, trying to project an air of calm while shouting above Oliver's incessant screaming. "Okay, we're done. You can go to Daddy as soon as he takes off his shirt."

I allowed a flush of modesty to briefly color my cheeks, before reflecting on what Madisyn had just gone through. If she could expose the inside of her uterus to an entire roomful of people, I could easily take off my shirt in front a nurse.

After removing the blue smock, I sat in a padded chair, and she gently placed the naked baby onto my bare chest. He was still crying, but for the first time in my life the sound didn't bother me. I had always found the wail of a baby akin to fingernails on a chalkboard, but when my own flesh and blood was screaming within inches of my ear, I only wanted to comfort him.

"Put your arms around him and support his head," the nurse instructed as she covered us both with a large blanket. "He wants to feel your warmth—skin-to-skin."

I gently cradled him by crossing both my arms around his newborn body and repeatedly kissed the crown of his head. As I instinctively rocked him back and forth, his cries began to wane, and within a few short seconds he was completely silent.

"I'm turning off the lights," whispered the nurse as she flipped the wall switch, "and I'll go check on Mommy so you can both have some time to get to know each other."

Once we had been left alone, I became acutely aware of his tiny heartbeat tapping rapidly next to my own. As I listened with my entire body, it was easy to lose myself in the smoothness of his flawless pink skin and the rhythm of the tiny puffs of air he expelled from his newly functioning lungs with every shallow breath.

In the bliss of that moment I became aware of a grain-sized seed of light that sprouted from our collective hearts and began to grow. The energy was warm and nurturing, and once it had enveloped us completely, it gracefully turned on its axis and continued to expand into other dimensions. The light carried us on a journey along the Möbius strip of time, which cleverly folded in on itself and revealed that our souls were eternally facing each other.

It was then that I tasted the very essence of time itself and viscerally felt a deep connection with everything that was alive, everything that had ever lived before, and everything that would eventually exist. I realized that I had never truly understood my own relationship to subsequent generations and had always coped with a mental construct of time that was fiercely limited. But by holding my newborn child in my arms, I was finally able to palpably feel *the future* in every one of my cells.

My epiphany seemed to enliven my son, and for the first time in his life, he opened his almond-shaped eyes and looked at me intently.

"Nice to meet you, Oliver Moon," I said softly. "I'm your father, and I'm so glad you're finally here."

EPILOGUE

"Do you want to go to the medicine wheel?" asked Madisyn on an exceptionally beautiful spring day a few weeks after we had returned home from the hospital.

Some friends of ours had discovered an ancient medicine wheel that had remained hidden for decades near the peak of Mount Ashland. They had carefully restored the sacred site and occasionally shared its location with a few lucky people, whom we were fortunate to be among. Madisyn and I both found it to be one of the most profoundly rejuvenating places in southern Oregon, and reserved our time there for when we needed it most.

"I don't know if the snow has completely melted," I replied, "but we can drive as far as we're able and hike the rest of the way to the trailhead. Today would be a perfect day for Oliver to discover the joys of being in nature."

During the whirlwind of activity throughout the previous several weeks, we had been unable to fully appreciate the changing of the seasons. Ashland had always been one of my favorite places to be in the springtime, and as we drove out of town toward the freeway, I reveled in the beauty of the flowers that remained in bloom along the boulevard.

After exiting the freeway and driving along the base of the mountain, we were able to make it most of the way up the unmarked dirt road with our four-wheel drive before a large snowdrift prevented us from continuing onward. Fortunately, we safely navigated our way to an open clearing, where we parked the car.

"Are you sure you're up for hiking the rest of the way?" I asked. Although Madisyn was feeling much better than she had been before the birth, I was still mindful that she hadn't fully recovered from major surgery.

"I really need to go," she replied. "I haven't had a meaningful connection with nature in almost a year."

I fumbled with the front-loading baby carrier, trying to remember which strap went where. Although I had given it a practice run at the house, this was the first time I had attempted to use it in the real world. Thankfully, Oliver was uncharacteristically patient with me as I threaded his tiny arms and legs through their respective holes before buttoning him in. Once strapped in, he looked like a cross between an infant and a turtle, with his tiny arms and legs dangling out of the padded brown shell. The top of his head was barely visible, and his nose pressed tightly against my chest.

We hiked up the road as far as we could, although there were times when we needed to forge a detour after coming across a snowdrift that had remained perpetually shaded. At first it was nerve-racking to keep my balance while hiking up a slippery mountain road with a newborn strapped to my chest, but I began to enjoy the trek much more once we found footsteps in the snow that we were able to follow. The hike to the trailhead took much longer than expected, but after pausing a few times for Madisyn to get her breath, we all made it in good spirits.

"Look at that!" I gasped as we emerged from the darkened forest into a vast sunlit meadow. "Can you believe how beautiful it is this time of year?"

We had visited this very place on several occasions over the years, but this was the first time we had seen it so alive. The gently sloping field was completely covered in tiny blue wildflowers that swayed in the breeze as far as the eye could see. The sea of indigo stretched on for miles, and the air was filled with a pungent sweetness that smelled like a unique blend of French lavender and white sage.

My heart began to lighten as we meandered through the meadow and straddled a web of rivulets distributing the melting snow among the recently sprouted vegetation. There was something about this marshy game of hopscotch that seemed to erase our troubles and force us to focus on being present as a family of three. As we continued on our journey, I found myself kissing Oliver's silky chestnut hair every time my steps gently brought the top of his head to meet my lips.

"It's this way," called Madisyn, who was already several steps off the well-worn path. "You'd get lost in the wilderness for days if I wasn't with you."

I tried my best to come up with a credible rebuttal, but realized that she was at least partially right. She did have a much better sense of direction than I did, although my pesky Y chromosome oftentimes made that difficult to admit. After catching up with her, we came to a bluff that provided an exquisite view of the canyons below. Waiting for us beyond the imaginary border dividing Oregon from California was one of the most majestic natural wonders in North America. The clear blue sky kissed the top of stunning snow-capped Mount Shasta, and a single white cloud crowned Shastina, the mountain's own sister peak.

I turned sideways in order to make sure that the vista wouldn't be lost on my papoose. "What do you think of that, Mr. Moon?"

Our baby's eyes widened as he scanned the panoramic view, taking in as much as he could from his limited vantage point. After staring at the mountain for nearly a minute, he captured the magnificence perfectly with a single syllable: "Humph!"

Madisyn and I burst out laughing, as we were both in awe of our baby's eloquence. It was amazing to see the world through his eyes.

"Come on, we're nearly there," urged Madisyn as she led us a few hundred yards across the mesa to the edge of the ceremonial grounds.

The large medicine wheel comprised hundreds of rocks and pebbles meticulously arranged in the shape of a perfect circle that was divided into four quadrants. Each intersecting spoke was made by laying different-colored stones: reddish terra-cotta for the southern direction, pointing to the mountain; black for the west; white for the north; and yellowish brown for the east. In the hub of the wheel was a simple altar containing a collection of exotic specimens, including arrowheads, crystals, feathers, and the remains of a recently burned smudge stick.

"It looks like we aren't the first to visit this year," I said, noticing the mound of fresh ashes. "Whoever came here last was probably responsible for the footsteps in the snow we saw before."

I carefully unbuttoned the chocolate-brown carrier to release Oliver and dropped the tangle of padded straps to the ground.

"Keep him covered up," said Madisyn as she handed me a blanket from her rattan tote. "I'm going to the edge to find a rock to sit on."

"Don't you want to come into the medicine wheel?"

"Not today," she said. "Today, I need to be with the mountain."

Oliver and I watched as Madisyn slowly disappeared over the edge of the precipice. Although the canyon walls were steep, I knew that there were a few large boulders just over the edge before the terrain became too treacherous.

"I guess it's just you and me, kid," I whispered to Oliver as we began walking around the exterior edge of the wheel. After circling four times, we stopped outside the southeastern quadrant, and I took a deep breath. I could sense the energy pulsing from inside the circle, and when we stepped over the seemingly arbitrary line of stones, I felt as if I had entered the heart of a powerful electric generator. The hair on the back of my neck stood on end as the vibrant energetic current connected me to its powerful source.

I'd felt a similar sensation when I had visited the sacred site before, but then it had been much subtler. It was as if my son was a powerful conduit to the very source energy I was feeling, and somehow his presence amplified its power a hundredfold. My paternal instinct made me question whether it was safe to remain inside with a newborn; however, when I lifted him up, I could see in his eyes that not only was he obviously safe, but he was likely responsible for everything I was feeling.

After we sat down, Oliver was single-mindedly drawn to the center hub and attempted to grab for a specific item that caught his attention.

"Do you want this?" I asked as I picked up a small arrowhead that had been handmade from quartz crystal. The years had dulled its chipped edges, although the distinctive shape remained recognizably intact. My son eagerly grabbed the relic from my fingers and held it tightly in his closed fist. Somehow the talisman comforted him, and I took the opportunity to lie down on my back and position him facedown on my chest.

I closed my eyes, and as our energy joined together, I felt the serenity embodied within the arrowhead begin to flow through my child and into the crevices of my soul. There was no more separation between him and me, or the earth and the sky. We dissolved into each other and hovered simultaneously deep in the earth and high in the sky in a sublimely meditative state that had no beginning or end.

Then a powerful surge of energy entered my body through the soles of my feet. The force was so great that I felt my knees buckle, and when I opened my eyes, I saw Mount Shasta towering above us. Flowing from its snow-covered crevices was a river of opaline energy that tethered my feet to its mountainous heart center. The powerful force was so great that I felt more a part of the earth than I ever had before.

Simultaneously, the cloudless sky ripped open, and from within the atmospheric wound a beam of golden light shone brightly onto the back of my child and seeped into my chest. He filled me with divine light unlike anything I had ever felt before. My son connected me to Father Sky, and I connected him to Mother Earth. And together we combined to embody the entirety of the universe. In that moment of crystal clarity, I understood that we needed each other to be whole—we needed each other to be fully alive.

Gradually, the intensity began to fade, and once the rapturous energy had nearly dissipated, I sat up, bringing Oliver to me, nose to nose. As I looked deep into my son's sparkling blue eyes, I could sense that not only had he experienced everything I had, but he remained filled with the essence that came from both the sky and the mountain. I silently prayed that I could do the same.

Then he held out his tiny pillowed hand and uncurled his fingers to reveal the arrowhead that he had carefully protected during our divine encounter.

"Thank you," I said as I returned the artifact to the hub of the medicine wheel. As I closed my eyes again to meditate on everything that had just happened, Oliver began to fidget for the first time since we had entered the sacred grounds. He impatiently tugged my shirt collar, and once he got my attention, he raised his arm and pointed to the east.

At first I didn't see what he was pointing at, but I gradually discerned a familiar shape begin to emerge from the blinding glare of the field.

"Oh, it's a deer," I whispered as my son looked at me with wide eyes while continuing to point. My gaze returning to the animal, I gasped as I realized that it wasn't an ordinary deer. It was a *pure white* deer. From head to hoof, her fur was as white as snow. In my life I had seen thousands of the graceful animals, but I had never seen one so fair before.

The doe tentatively walked toward us until we were able to look into her large brown eyes. She then stood still and stared at Oliver intently while he returned her gaze. It was remarkable how they appeared to be having a conversation without making a sound.

Then in an instant, the white deer bounded away as soon as she heard rustling coming from the cliff. She was gone by the time Madisyn emerged from the edge of the canyon, slowly walking toward us.

After bowing to the altar, I quickly carried Oliver out of the medicine wheel and greeted my wife.

"Did you see that?" I asked excitedly. "The deer?"

Madisyn slowly shook her head, and a single tear rolled down her cheek. Without pause, Oliver reached up with his tiny fingers to wipe it away. And for the first time in his life, he smiled.

My son's smile beamed like sunshine, and its radiant warmth proceeded to dry every last one of my wife's tears. His toothless grin was as infectious as it was heartwarming, and within moments both Madisyn and I couldn't help but join in.

In that tender moment, I finally understood that not only had this precious child arrived to take care of my family . . .

He was here to take care of us all.

Tina Bolling

Madisyn Taylor, Scott Blum, and Oliver Moon

ABOUT THE AUTHOR

Scott Blum is the best-selling author of *Waiting for Autumn* and *Summer's Path* and the co-founder of the popular inspirational website DailyOM (**www.dailyom.com**). He is also a filmmaker and multimedia artist who has collaborated with several popular authors, musicians, and visual artists and has produced many critically acclaimed works, including writing and directing the feature film *Walk-In,* based on his book *Summer's Path.* Scott lives in the mountains of Ashland, Oregon, with his wife and business partner, Madisyn Taylor, and their son, Oliver Moon.

Website: **www.scottblum.net**

RESOURCES

DailyOM is the online resource that Scott Blum and his wife, Madisyn Taylor, co-founded together. It has become the premier destination for providing inspirational content, products, and courses around the globe from some of today's best-selling authors and luminaries.

www.dailyom.com

Madisyn Taylor is a best-selling author, the co-founder and Editor-in-Chief of DailyOM, and Scott Blum's beautiful and talented wife. Attentively combining soulful wisdom and inspired design, Madisyn nurtures a range of projects that revitalize the spirit, heal the body, and beautify the home. Each project is created not only to take advantage of all the best that nature and spirit have to offer, but to do so in a way that is aesthetically pleasing and visually graceful.

www.madisyntaylor.com

Andrew Harvey is an author, religious scholar, and teacher of mystic traditions, known primarily for his popular books on spiritual or mystical themes, beginning with his 1983 *A Journey in Ladakh.* He is the author of more than 30 books, including *The Hope: A Guide to Sacred Activism, The Sun at Midnight,* the critically acclaimed *The Way of Passion: A Celebration of Rumi, The Return of the Mother,* and *Son of Man.* Andrew was the subject of the 1993 BBC documentary *The Making of a Modern Mystic.* He is the founder of the Sacred Activism movement and serves as the director of the Institute of Sacred Activism.

www.andrewharvey.net

Marina McDonald is the founder and director of Movements of Love, an accelerated, highly experiential group process for personal, spiritual, and ancestral healing of traumas and entanglements. Resting on a foundation of Buddhist principles of compassion and nonviolence, Movements of Love is the result of carefully weaving together modern healing modalities with ancient indigenous technologies to offer a truly transformative experience of personal and planetary healing.

www.movementsoflove.org

Hay House Titles of Related Interest

YOU CAN HEAL YOUR LIFE, the movie,
starring Louise L. Hay & Friends
(available as a 1-DVD program and an expanded 2-DVD set)
Watch the trailer at: **www.LouiseHayMovie.com**

THE SHIFT, the movie,
starring Dr. Wayne W. Dyer
(available as a 1-DVD program and an expanded 2-DVD set)
Watch the trailer at: **www.DyerMovie.com**

DailyOM: Learning to Live, by Madisyn Taylor

THE GOLDEN MOTORCYCLE GANG: A Story of Transformation, by Jack Canfield and William Gladstone

THE HIDDEN POWER OF YOUR PAST LIVES: Revealing Your Encoded Consciousness,
by Sandra Anne Taylor (book-with-CD)

THE HOPE: A Guide to Sacred Activism, by Andrew Harvey

LION EYES, by Victor Villaseñor

All of the above are available at your local bookstore,
or may be ordered by contacting Hay House (see next page).

We hope you enjoyed this Hay House book. If you'd like to receive our online catalog featuring additional information on Hay House books and products, or if you'd like to find out more about the Hay Foundation, please contact:

Hay House, Inc.,
P.O. Box 5100, Carlsbad, CA 92018-5100

(760) 431-7695 or (800) 654-5126
(760) 431-6948 (fax) or (800) 650-5115 (fax)
www.hayhouse.com® • www.hayfoundation.org

Published and distributed in Australia by:
Hay House Australia Pty. Ltd., 18/36 Ralph St., Alexandria NSW 2015
Phone: 612-9669-4299 • *Fax:* 612-9669-4144 • www.hayhouse.com.au

Published and distributed in the United Kingdom by:
Hay House UK, Ltd., 292B Kensal Rd., London W10 5BE
Phone: 44-20-8962-1230 • *Fax:* 44-20-8962-1239 • www.hayhouse.co.uk

Published and distributed in the Republic of South Africa by:
Hay House SA (Pty), Ltd., P.O. Box 990, Witkoppen 2068
Phone/Fax: 27-11-467-8904 • www.hayhouse.co.za

Published in India by: Hay House Publishers India,
Muskaan Complex, Plot No. 3, B-2, Vasant Kunj, New Delhi 110 070
Phone: 91-11-4176-1620 • *Fax:* 91-11-4176-1630 • www.hayhouse.co.in

Distributed in Canada by:
Raincoast, 9050 Shaughnessy St., Vancouver, B.C. V6P 6E5
Phone: (604) 323-7100 • *Fax:* (604) 323-2600 • www.raincoast.com

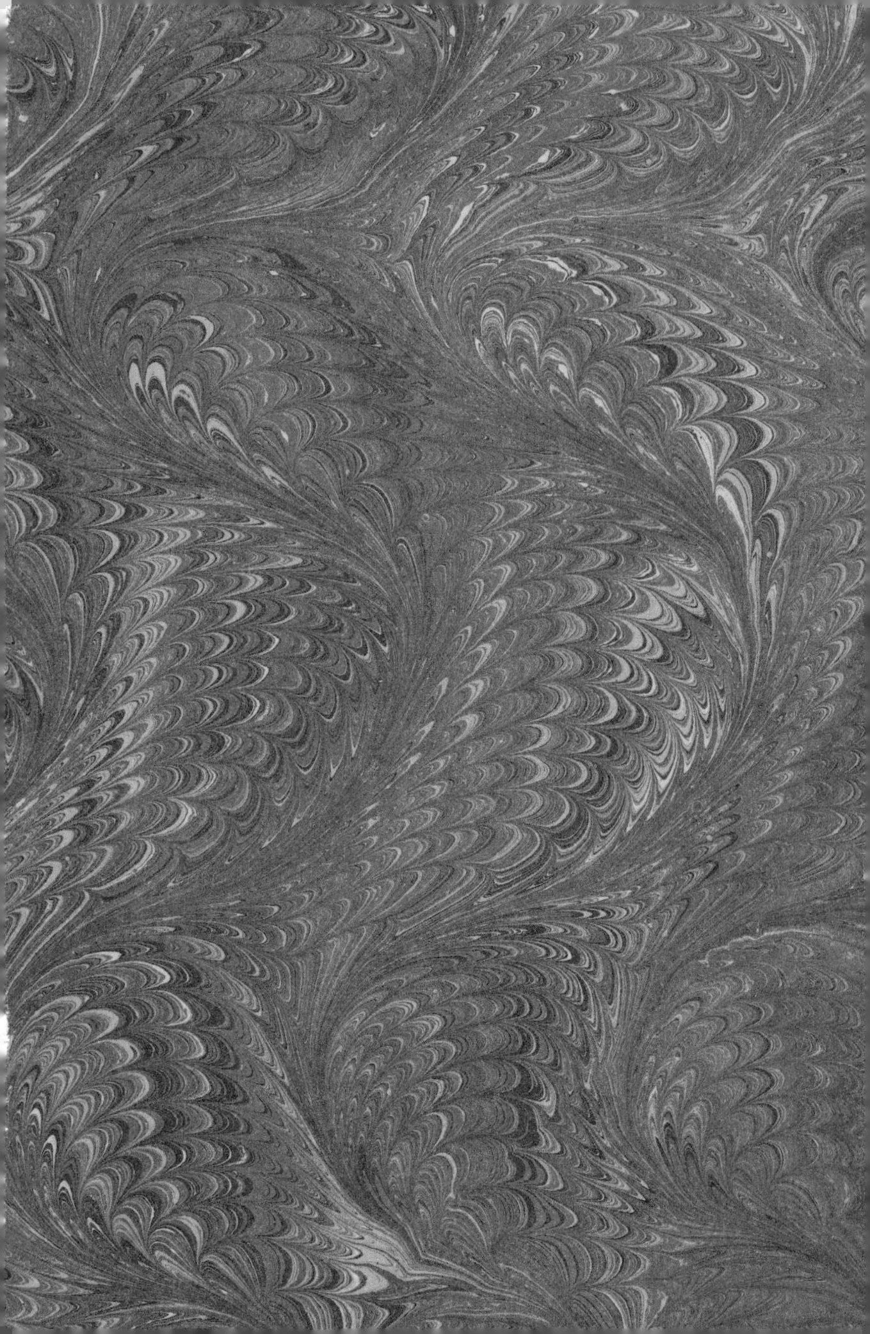

This certifies that

____

Child of ________________________________

and ____________________________________

born in _________________________________

on the ________ *day of* ____________ *19* _____

was Baptized

on the ________ *day of* ____________ *19* _____

According to the Rite of the

Roman Catholic Church

by the Rev. ______________________________

Godparents ______________________________

____

as recorded on the Baptismal

Register of this Church,

____

Dated _______________ *19* _____

Rev. ___________________________________